MONKEY

IN

A TREE

A NOVEL

by

Rodger Christopherson

Other books by the author:

A Little Bit of Anarchy
Out of the Fire Mist
Beverly Hills Women
Health and the Real Cause of Illness
Beyond Science and Religion - The Greater Reality
After the President Disappeared
Three Weeks Until Tomorrow
Illusions
How Science and Religion Failed Humanity - non fiction
Tears and Hope - Poetry

intercept777@centurylink.net

MONKEY IN A TREE

ONE

Dr. Jill Kairns stood on a low rise overlooking the immense, almost endless white landscape, pushed back the hood of her down filled parka and shook out her long blond hair. Full circle, the ice was melting. Everywhere little trickles of water were merging, growing in size and flowing faster and faster as they ran their descending, zig zagged courses over the frozen surface, headed towards the sea.

Moving carefully to keep from falling, she made her way slowly downward, knowing full well that it wasn't wise for her to be out there wandering around alone like a fool. This was Antarctica, for god's sake. Five and a half million square miles of cold and treacherous unpredictability. But she had left base camp anyway, feeling the need for solitude to think things through.

Something was seriously wrong. They had re calibrated all their instrumentation half a dozen times and yet the data was always the same. Extreme and nearly impossible to believe. How could things have gotten so bad in such a short period of time? Well, hopefully, they would soon know for sure. The flight data from three other stations around the southern pole would start coming in tomorrow and the failed synchronous satellite overhead was up and running again and ready for interrogation. And if it all agreed and confirmed their own findings, what then, she wondered as her cautious footsteps finally took her to the cliff like edge of the ice sheet, the sharp demarcation between the stark white covering of the land and the deep, icy blue of the ocean far below.

The implications of what was happening were most ominous. Not only had the western ice sheet almost fully collapsed and ocean levels risen more than five feet since the beginning of global warming, the major sheet was disappearing three times faster than predicted just ten years earlier. And what would another ten bring? But disappearing coastlines were one thing. The way their data gathering expedition seemed to be turning out was something else again. The phytoplankton densities in the Weddell Sea were down sixty percent in the last five years alone and the dependent, crab-like krill population was down nearly fifty percent with the reduced counts extending on up through the food chain as a result. Whales, squid, seals and penguins were all in serious trouble. Ultimately, so were humans, along with every other living thing on the entire planet.

"Damn," she said, swearing out loud before realizing how much time must have gone by. She had better get her head covered and get back to camp before the short wavelength radiation did a number on her too.

Hood up, she took one last glance out over the ocean, turned and started back up the incline. Finally concerned about her own safety, she increased her pace, only to slip and fall, bruising both knees in the process. Ignoring the pain as best she could, she finally got up, only to be startled by an ear shattering, sharp crackling boom that pierced the air from behind as the ground shuddered and frightened her into slipping again. Falling, she turned just in time to see the entire ledge of ice she had just walked across dropping away into the ocean far below, carrying the awesome rumble downward with it. Then, long moments later, another sound filled the air as a mass of ice blue, churning water rose more than fifty feet above the newly generated, sharp edge of the ice sheet where Jill lay helplessly sprawled. It hung there like some strange, foreboding hobgoblin of the sea, suspended in space for what seemed a near eternity with its own symbolic message, then slowly dropped back into the ocean from whence it had come.

TWO

Sam Gorhman stood on the bluff overlooking the palisades along the Santa Monica waterfront and stared out at the bay and what remained of the beach. Not very much anymore, now that the city had given up trying to save it. Couldn't afford the expense. Not since the "big one." The eight point seven that had reverberated down the San Andreas fault four years earlier and wiped out the cities of Palmdale and Lancaster, moved into Los Angeles and leveled half the downtown area along with a good portion of Pasadena and parts of Orange County. Even Disneyland of all things, had been destroyed in the disaster. And now hurricanes were coming ashore along the west coast too, to add to the misery and a death toll that was already staggering. So who cared about a few miles of beach which had almost entirely yielded to rising waters and higher tides along the coast at a time like this? Not very many, to be sure. No one that he knew of. Except for himself. He cared.

Damned right. His love of the beach was a personal thing. Those beautiful days when he used to park his car along Ocean Avenue a little farther up, walk down the one hundred and forty two wooden steps from the park to the pad below, take the overpass across the highway, down another thirty two steps to the parking lot, over to the sand. Sand nearly a quarter mile wide back then, soft sand, warm in the sunlight. A bright, ornamental ribbon of white that stretched on down the coast nearly to Palos Verde, ended at the hills, picked itself up again on around the peninsula and skipped its way clear to San Diego, over a hundred miles away.

Good exercise, walking in the sand. Good for the legs. Good for him at a time when he needed it. Walk the two miles down the beach to the pier, avoid the trash, try not to step on any washed up tar from old oil spills, avoid the inner city kids throwing mud at each other, ignore the camera laden foreigners. Listen to the surf, watch the gulls, look at the girls, drink a beer, take the road back up to the park, pick your way through the old, retired folks bumbling around, don't step on the homeless sleeping on the grass, mind your own business and back to the car. Approximately four miles in all. Do it four or five times a week and it made you feel at least partially alive. But not anymore. Too late for that.

Except for an isolated bit of beach here and there, the sand was mostly gone, covered up with debris or washed away. Still, however, if they tore down that dumpy old pier, pushed a little more dirt down the hill to hide the rest of the crumbling asphalt of the old Pacific Coast Highway, put a match to what was left of the Marathon Club and the row of decrepit, partially submerged buildings alongside, it might not be too bad. Or give it another ten years or so. Let nature finish taking it's course. A couple more feet of sea water, high tides and strong surf and it would all be swept clean away. What man can do, nature can undo, even more effectively.

Tragic as that might be for humans, sooner or later nature would prevail and when it finally did, perhaps then the southern California coastline would be beautiful again. Until then, however.... and with that Sam shrugged and started to turn away just as a lone seagull appeared in the sky, turned and glided near, then hung there in the air above him, working the off shore breeze to maintain his position while sharing the same bleak sight. Did he know too, what it had been like before? Sam wondered. Was there something buried in his genes, some biological memory of better days passed along from bird to egg to bird? Or was he just looking for a handout like the bums that lived their shadowy, semi existence sleeping in the bushes here in the park, shunned by the rest of society. Perhaps if they had wings like the bird... Perhaps if he had wings like a bird...

The yellow billed, white gull eyeballed him intently so he held out his empty hand, open palm upward, signifying that he had nothing to offer. The bird looked carefully, turned its head as if in apparent comprehension, changed the angle and pitch of its wings, did a slight left roll and glided downward, back towards the sea below. Sam smiled at the intelligence it had displayed and wished he could join it in some brief flight of

6

freedom.

Freedom, that was the thing. So who told him he could write and how the hell did he ever end up being an investigative reporter anyway? Especially for such a biased, half assed rag sheet as the Los Angeles Mirror for christsake? And, damn. Speaking of his employer, he supposed it was about time he stopped thinking about seagulls and the quickly deteriorating state of the beach and put in an appearance at his office for a change.

Busy with her notes, Julie failed to look up when she heard the elevator door open as Sam got off and headed down the hall and he was well past her before she realized who it was. Even then she nearly didn't speak. It wasn't that she was afraid of him. Not exactly, anyway. Mostly, she just didn't understand him. He was so unlike the rest of the men she knew and, as a result, she found him difficult to deal with. He was too independent for one thing. Made up his own rules, the shit. And worse, if he didn't want to play bedroom games with her, there was no way to make him, slinky feminine charm or not.

To her, Sam was one of the best looking men she had ever met. When she first started working there a year ago she saw him as a delightful conquest and set out in seductive earnest to do him in. But it hadn't worked. Sam still remained out of reach. And that was just wrong. Men didn't reject her, she was the one who decided such things. How could he have done that to her, she wondered, and resented it.

Sam was almost out of hearing range before she finally spoke. "Mr. Gorhman," she said, using this formal way of addressing Sam to let him know she still thought he was a bit of a snob and a rat for not wanting to pursue her sexy charm.

His thoughts interrupted, Sam turned. Ignoring the "Mr. Gorhman" part he walked back towards her desk, looking at her as he went, allowing his eyes and his mind to roam over her obvious proportions. She was a sexy female all right, physically speaking. And he wondered about all about the wild motion and passionate commotion that might follow when buttons were unbuttoned and all that great flesh was exposed.

But that was as far as it went because he otherwise thought of her as conniving, contriving and very self centered, lacking in the more important qualities he needed before getting involved. Regardless, there were times when it was still tempting, to be sure. Damn right, he decided as he looked her over once again.

"Mr. Barnes wants to see you right away," she said when he was closer, a polite, hesitant, almost smile on her face for a change which rather surprised him.

"Really," said Sam.

"Should I let him know you're here?"

"No. I need to get some coffee first,"

"I think he's pretty upset."

Sam shrugged and smiled but said nothing. Julie was also surprisingly silent for a change and avoided the direct look of his eyes as he studied her face, noting the subdued look and the refreshing lack of response. What's this? he wondered. Maybe she had changed. He acknowledged the thought and filed it away.

"Thanks Julie," he said rather nicely for once, took one last look, turned and walked back in the direction he came from.

Half an hour later Cliff Barnes stormed into his office. "Where the hell have you been for the last three days?" he demanded to know.

Sam swiveled around in his chair, reached for his coffee cup, leaned back and looked up at Cliff's fleshy, pallid mug with all its disproportionate protrusions. If ever a man needed to let his hair grow, it was Cliff. Those big ears could keep an elephant airborne. Except for that minor defect however, they were still part of Cliff's more pleasant characteristics. How did I wind up working for this fool? Sam wondered as he looked at him, knowing full well how it had happened. "I thought I was supposed to be an investigative reporter?" he said instead, sounding innocent enough.

"I believe that's your title," Cliff replied sarcastically.

Cliff had been Editor in Chief of a large, national women's magazine until it had folded six months earlier, his own short-comings contributing heavily to its painful demise. Fortunately however, he had had enough sense to have married the owner of the Los Angeles Mirror's oldest, and equally desperate daughter shortly before that happened and wound up with his present job at the west coast's largest newspaper. His new title was International Editor, something which was designed to cover whatever it was that his new father-in-law, Hudson Soloman, trusted him with at the moment. Actually, when it came right down to it the old man wasn't too worried because Cliff's staff still had some good people left on it, including Sam, whom he'd had to make some exorbitant financial concessions to, to keep.

"Well, maybe you can do your job from behind a desk," Sam said. "But somehow I'm not able to do much fact finding sitting on my duff in this stuffy, airless little closet you claim is an office."

"You might try and call in once in a while."

"I do," Sam said. "When I have something to report."

"What if I need something?"

"Leave me a note, put a message on my computer, tell Julie."

"I did all three, plus you're damned cell phone which is always turned off, and you still ignored me."

"I'm here now. What do you want?"

"I want you to go to New York."

New York? Good grief, Sam said to himself. What about Russia and Brazil, dammit? Three months he'd been asking for that assignment. Something very sinister was going on in those two countries. He had his own ideas as to what, or who, was behind it and he wanted a chance to find out. Whatever it was, he was convinced that it would be something noteworthy for a change. He reminded Cliff of it once again. Once again Cliff negated it.

"Guess I should have taken that job with the Washington Post," Sam said for the second time in the last few days just to agitate Cliff. "They would have let me do it."

Cliff ignored him, staring at the papers on Sam's desk, trying to read them upside down.

"All right," Sam said at last.

But then, as he was agreeing, his thoughts turned to a woman named Schalla. Ah yes, Schalla. Schalla lived in New York, didn't she? Now there was a female who had some depth. He didn't know about the sex because they hadn't crossed that line but she certainly was enjoyable to be with in every other sense of the word. So, what the hell. Why not?

"What's in New York?" he asked.

"We'd like to know what's happening with UNACC and what kind of progress they've made. Maybe a little update for the general public," Cliff said.

Sam looked at him incredulously. UNACC? UNACC was the impressively named United Nations Atmospheric Control Council, an organization established shortly after the latest war in the middle east when all the oil fields went up in smoke for the second time in history, rapidly accelerating the greenhouse effect.

"An update for who?" he asked with a scoff.

"The public. Those persons who still buy newspapers and subscribe on-line. And try to keep it informative and light for a change. People are tired of hearing bad news all the time."

Sam sighed. "You've spent too many years purveying pantyhose and pancake makeup, Cliff," he said. "The world doesn't need a softer toilet tissue, it needs a harder kick in the ass, especially now while there's still some of it left to kick."

"Our function is to report the news in an unbiased fashion, not to keep the public stirred up by insulting every world leader around the globe, along with the president and congress and every other governmental agency there is."

"Why? Do you think the public is some innocent little group of bystanders off in the corner somewhere that needs to be kept in the dark and life is just a fun little game without any consequences?"

"No. But UNACC is vital and its chairman, Dr. Rouard is an important man. The public likes him and if the world is going to be saved, he's going to play a big part in it. Go a little easy on him, that's all I ask."

"Right. Let's play poker with match sticks and gin rummy for buttons, too, while we're at it. Is that what you're saying? Christ, Cliff, did you forget the statistics? The world has lost nearly half a billion people in the last ten years, due almost entirely to greenhouse related effects on world climate."

"Do you have to remind me all the time? It's very depressing."

"Yes, it must be tough for you," Sam said, knowing Cliff didn't have any first hand experience with tragedy. He hadn't even been in L.A. when the big quake hit. No, he was cooling his buns in some plush mountain resort at the time instead. Stayed there six weeks, the little wimp, instead of returning to help. He knew nothing about life, or suffering, or people.

Sam did, however. He was the one who had treaded through the sands of Africa, the dust and filth of India, the desolation of South America. It was he who had seen the eroding landscapes and looked into the faces of the starving and the dying. It was he who had seen the piles of bones more than a city block long lying in the sun. And it was his rather gruesome series of articles that had finally stirred up enough national concern to get the government to put forward a substantial portion of funding devoted strictly to problem solving solutions. Unfortunately it was still far too little. And far too late.

But that was normal. Like most of the worlds tragedies, the US. was to a large extent, still isolated from the deepest part of it. Sure, the plains states were blowing away in the wind, half of Los Angeles had been leveled by the shaking ground and the lower end of Florida and other coastal areas were disappearing under water but other than that, life went on. Money and status were still king.

And then, after all that effort on his part to get congress to give more funding to FEMA, the Army Corps of Engineers and other agencies that might provide some real help to the unfortunate victims of changing weather problems, horror of horrors. Who did the bumbling bureaucrats give most of the

11

money to? Why UNACC, of course. Dr. Pierre Rouard to be more specific. Doctor Dimbulb Fuckhead, scientific whistle ass. For some illogical reason they had just handed him all that money with no control over the use of the funds or without establishing milestones of accomplishment. Would they never learn?

Sam thought of taking a few more verbal swipes at Cliff but let it go. Why bother? He would go to New York, not for the distasteful story he would be compelled to write about but to have a good time. Hopefully, Schalla was still uninvolved.

THREE

"Take the pig too, Will."

"I can't, Bud. I can't pay you for it."

"Doesn't matter."

"Does to me. I can't pay you."

"It's only money, dammit. The pig needs a home too. Can't stay here by itself. It'll die."

"Well, maybe I can send you something when it's big enough for market."

"Don't worry about it," Bud said, his thoughtful blue eyes on the grizzled, leathery face.

"Come on, give me a hand."

The two men, Bud and Will, wading through the mud and shit, backed the animal into the corner of the pig pen, grabbed the forty two pounds of squealing, squirming, impossible to hang onto pile of lard and hauled him away. Bud, the younger man on the front and Will, gnarled, older looking than the falling down barn but tougher than the oak tree in the yard, grabbing the rear. Off to Will's old and sagging, stake bed truck. In went the pig to fend for himself beneath the feet of the two milk cows already aboard. Will closed the tailgate, wiped his hands on his jeans and scraped the muck off his boots on the rear bumper of the truck.

"Well, partner. Good luck," he said, sadly and seriously. "And thanks. Drop me and Gracie a line when you get where you're going."

"We will."

Bud extended his hand. They shook. Strong, hard, heavily callused hands coming together, firmly but briefly communicating without words. A long friendship, better times, other times, shared struggles with the land, the drought, the banks, the government. Good-bye old timer. Good-bye young friend.

Will climbed into the cab, pulled the windowless door shut with a clang. The starter whined, gear teeth clashed, the engine turned over, coughed, caught. A puff of blue smoke rose from the exhaust. A starting lurch sent the animals up against the tail gate as Will let out the clutch and they were on their way. Bud heard the screen door slam behind him. He turned. Jean came running from the house, her long straight, dark hair flying, waving at the departing truck.

"Good-bye Mr. Jenson," she yelled.

Jenson's arm showed out the windowless window of the truck. He waved back, slowed a bit for the rut in the dirt drive, then stepped on the gas. Bud put his arm around his wife, trying not to soil her dress. They watched the battered old truck fade away down the long driveway, reach the old blacktopped highway, turn left and disappear.

"Well, no chores to do tonight," Bud said.

Jean looked up at him and studied his face. She sensed his sadness even though he kept it well hidden. She turned to the western sky.

"I think we're going to have a nice sunset," she said instead, trying to be cheerful. Then she looked back at Bud, her husband, friend and lover for the last six years, the man who owned her heart. "Let's take a last look around before dinner," she said rather pensively.

"Let me rinse off first," he answered.

They walked to the quarter full watering tank standing next to the bent and bedraggled looking old windmill. Jean helped Bud roll up the sleeves of his shirt. Bud brushed the light scum off the water's surface and scrubbed his hands in the water, flipped them a couple of times to shake off the excess moisture and took her small, delicately shaped, dry hand in his huge wet one. They started off, heading in a direction that would take them around the barn and out into the field beyond, the field of small, dried, bent stalks of corn which never got to rise more than a foot above the hard, baked soil. There were forty acres of crop in there, all dead now from lack of rain. They tried not to look at it as they made there way down the smoother edge of the long field.

At the end of the field, Bud put his boot on the lower strand of barbed wire and pushed it down while holding up the middle one with his hands. Jean bundled her skirt around her and slipped through the opening. Bud followed. They were soon at the creek bed, normally flowing at this time of year. Now however, there were only a few scattered, shallow puddles of water remaining. No pollywogs either and except for a few mosquito larvae, the pools were completely lifeless. The solitary survivor in the scene was a small willow tree, still green and beautiful, roots deep into the ground, arched branches shimmering lightly in the evening breeze, a small carpet of grass and weeds still semi verdant at its feet.

Bud sat down on the grass and spread his knees. Jean collapsed between them and leaned back against his broad chest. He put his arms around her, head forward over her shoulder, his cheek touching hers and squeezed her tight. The sun was down on the rim of the world and the powers that be were stirring the sky, adding colors, changing hues, stretching the proportions, keeping it alive as long as possible in the silent end of the day. Beauty and sadness. It was to be their last day on the farm, their home since they had graduated from college and gotten married. One year of hope, six years of pain and struggle. Tomorrow, gone forever, theirs no more.

Thank god for Jean, Bud thought to himself. He kissed her cheek and nuzzled her hair. High, proud cheekbones, long straight, luxurious, shining, halfway to her waist, dark hair. Dark and warm as her eyes, reflecting that small percentage of her American Indian heritage that was native to these same plains, generations past in more simpler times. Jean reacted to the kiss with a slight movement of her head. Bud moved his hands up, cupped her breasts and kissed her neck. Jean sighed, turned her head more, kissed him on the mouth.

Soon their clothes were spread evenly on the ground, a blanket for Jean, the following act an expression of love, courage, hope, trust and an affirmation of the bond between them. Wherever they went, they would go together. Whatever they did, they would do it together. Somehow they would survive.

FOUR

The ferry boat captain cut back the throttle of the big jet engine mounted topside. Losing speed and lift from its hydrofoil, the long, sleek, fluid born craft slowly dropped its main hull back into the water and glided gracefully into the harbor and up to the dock. Jill got off the Watson's Bay boat at the Sydney Circular Quay, freed herself from the crowd and started up the inclined walkway to George Street. Before turning right at the top she stopped to look back at the scene below. The Opera Center, Sydney's controversial, but grandly renowned international symbol, more striking than ever in the morning sun, sitting on its pedestal.

Fortunately the disgruntled Dane who had designed it had placed the main structure high enough above the waters of the bay to survive the inundation thus far. Although all the lower shops and offices were flooded, the main building was still high and dry, accessed now by a footbridge from the shoreline. Inside the structure the huge clam shell roof sections arced skyward with their original integrity and the worlds largest pipe organ still played vibrant and true, reverberating off the flawless acoustical innards of the main auditorium twice weekly.

Regardless, Jill wasn't particularly pleased to be back in Sydney but it was the only place where the reams of collected data could be processed, correlated and up-linked to the rest of the world. Hopefully Ernie would have a good share of the tedium completed by the time she arrived. She continued up the street, fighting here way through the early morning, big city rush. Different now, however, these last several years.

15

Aussie men no longer wore their traditional shorts and sport shirts. Now it was long pants, long sleeved shirts and wide brimmed hats. For the women, sun umbrellas had become mandatory, along with more time spent undercover. Indoor sports, television and drinking had become the new lifestyle.

Drinking in particular, had become the real national pastime as anyone who had ever walked past Molly Malones, or any of the dozens of other bars, saloons or restaurants along George Street, would attest to. Even at seven thirty in the morning the place was nearly standing room only. The noise followed her down the street to her own acid rain etched, dirty windowed old stone headquarters building and turned the corner with her, a brief, half second long chunk of it sneaking through the door when she opened it, only to be cut off when she closed the thick wooden barrier and went down the hall to the data processing room.

Ernie was busy arranging multi-channel strip chart recordings on the large work table in the center of the room, already perspiring in the rising humidity of what would be another hot, sticky day. Paper strips that were an antiquated way of data storage but still an effective one for what they were doing.

"Morning. Welcome back," he said to her, looking over his glasses, smiling, liking his job even more now that she was back in town. No way should such a lovely creature as her be out there tramping through the snow and ice of the Antarctic, the heat and sand of the outback or any of those other remote, god-for-saken places where research camps tend to be located.

"Thanks Ernie. Some pile of paper you have there. Anything interesting?"

"Distressing is more the word. Just as you predicted," He said and permitted himself another peak at her since it was one of the rare times he had seen her in a dress. A lady like that needs a man in her life, he thought in a semi-protective, older brother way, mixed with a tinge of something else that his own stable, happily married self kept well suppressed.

"Let's have a look," she said.

Ernie made a few last adjustments in the order of the long

paper strips, scratched his receding hairline and began. Here's Antarctic groundbase One and Two, overflight One and Two, Chile number One and Two, South Africa number One. Number Two still hasn't gotten off the ground. Poor buggers are up to their bloody knickers in rain water."

Jill pushed her long hair back over her shoulder and scanned the intricate rows of data, moving the charts around, comparing one to the other as Ernie's long, lanky body leaned over the table beside her, waiting to assist. "And the CFC satellites?"

"They confirm the whole miserable set," he said.

"Is the planet overview current?"

"It's all been entered. Should be digested by now."

Ernie followed her into the still darkened, adjoining room. Jill touched the light switch, moved across the room in the fluorescent flicker where they stopped at a keyboard on a floor stand in front of the opposite wall. Ernie punched in a code. Instantly, the entire wall turned into a floor to ceiling, full colored, modified polar projection of the earth, containing a series of coded, roughly concentric, irregular rings resembling isobars, centered around the south pole but displaying the entire southern hemisphere. Above the wall screen a large digital clock displayed the time and date. Eight fifty three and thirty seven seconds. Eleven, April, two thousand twenty six.

Jill stepped back and pulled at her chin. "Dammit, it's even worse than I thought," she said. "How does it compare to previous projections?"

"How far back do you want to go?"

"Six months, then a year."

"Let me see if I can coax it out of this thing," Ernie said and entered more data into the keyboard. The old circles vanished, replaced by new, differently located ones. They studied the display briefly before he repeated the process, then again, going back another six months. They looked at each other.

"Can you do a radial line section from the pole?" Jill asked. Maybe one through South America and another through

Australia? Do a time versus density profile?"

Ernie's fingers danced across the keyboard. The wall map disappeared, replaced by two large graphs showing the upper atmospheric ozone concentration as a function of distance from the south pole northward through South America and Australia clear to the equator with tagged plots for the various dates.

"Oh damn," Jill said, pulling at her chin.

Ernie looked glumly at the information and shook his head.

"Kill the second plot, take the first one and do a slow rotation around the pole ."

Complying, Ernie worked the keyboard some more. This time it took a little longer. A gradually changing, angular notation appeared on the screen along with the changing profile of the curve as it increased from zero to three sixty.

"All bad," he said.

"Stop somewhere and do a math curve fit."

More fingers on the keys, more information on the screen. Equations this time.

"It is, isn't it?" asked Jill.

"I'm afraid so," replied Ernie.

"Damn," Jill said loudly. "It doesn't make any sense. Let's pull up the north pole data again."

"No it doesn't," Ernie agreed after they examined the northern hemisphere information that had been gathered just the week before Jill had been in the antarctic. "This is really weird. Our equipment couldn't be that far off, could it?"

"Absolutely not. Same instrumentation, same calibration procedures. The data has to be correct."

"I know but how could it be? Almost zero north pole change and something akin to runaway at the south. Like you said, it makes no sense."

"No it doesn't. But we know it's correct. Look what's happening to the sea life there."

"And the penguins."

"And the penguins. Damn. Holy damn," Jill stated with emphasis and with that went to an intercom box on the wall, depressed the small button and spoke. "Emily, see if you can reach Doctor Rouard."

"Uh--It's evening in New York, Doctor Kairns. He probably won't be in his office."

"I know. Track him down. Call his cell phone."

FIVE

"I'm so glad you could make it, Sam. There's no one I would rather be here with than you," she said, referring to the black tie affair they were attending which she had been invited to some weeks back, an event that even the dire world situation couldn't dampen.

"Well, thank you. It's my pleasure," he said, quite impressed with the front table they were at and placed his arm over the back of her chair.

Schalla smiled and rested her hand gently on his knee as he covered it with his own. Then he leaned toward her, gave her a small kiss on the cheek and stole a look at the luxury of what her black sequined, strapless sheath of a dress was unable to hide. What more could a man want? he asked himself. She was intelligent, charming and beautiful. With her in his life he might even stop being so concerned about the world's problems and be willing to give up his globe trotting adventures. But would he be able to do such a thing and still be at peace with himself? If they got to know each other better would he care enough to do that? He wasn't sure as his thoughts came back to the speaker who ended the accolade he was engaged in, complimenting the officials of the charitable organization that was sponsoring the event. That over, Schalla's and Sam's hands returned to the scene above the table and they clapped. As the applause died, Sam excused himself, rose and headed out through the heavy oaken ballroom doors and down the hall to the men's room.

Far across the chandeliered and elegantly appointed ballroom at another table much farther back from the main floor than Schalla's and Sam's, a cell phone beeper sounded inside someone's pocket.

"Somebody's got a lot of nerve," said the pompous, portly, pile of a man, poorly dressed in an ill fitting tux which carried the intruding electronic device.

His mistress, younger, too much makeup, gaudy and overdone with cheap jewelry, leaned towards him.

"I hope it's not your wife," she said in a subdued voice that was still half scratch and half screech.

Doctor Pierre Rouard removed the device from his pocket and looked at the phone number registered on the display and then at the number of bars it showed. Not good. He'd have to find a better connection.

"Business, my dear. No rest for the gifted," he said to her, rising, looking down at her immense cleavage as he did so. "Back in a wink."

Sam finished drying his hands on the soft white hand towel, tossed it in the basket and left the men's room. Outside he passed the row of open phone booths along the wall. They didn't have pay phones in them anymore, however, just adapters which allowed a person to connect their cell phones directly to a land line for better reception where he overheard Rouard talking in an excited voice. "What do you mean, it's gone non linear?" the fat man was saying.

Well, Sam said to himself. There's the devil, himself. Didn't know the old fool was here. Wonder what he's shouting about? Sam went to the adjacent booth, turned so he wouldn't be recognized and pretended to make a call.

"Dammit Jill," Rouard went on. "I can't accept that. It's not even possible...What?...All right, let me see the data. But put it on the scrambler. My eyes only. And it stays confidential until you hear from me. Do you understand?"

With that Rouard ended his call, put his fat little hand in his pocket, took out his somewhat soiled handkerchief, mopped his puffy blob of a face and glanced briefly at the semi-hidden form in the next booth. Failing to recognize the back of the man next to him, he turned and walked back towards the ballroom.

The outer office of Doctor Rouard's was as overburdened as the man. A U N Flag in the corner, placards on the walls, office machines, chairs and table, books and periodicals piled everywhere, souvenirs, plants on oversized plant stands, paraphernalia and other things unasked for, unwanted and unused but all off limits to the comely, middle aged secretary who sat behind the old wooden desk typing a letter. Completing the one page document, she embellished it with a few corrections, reread it again, and printed a copy. Picking it up, she made a face, tore the sheet in two and threw it in the wastebasket. She was reaching for the keyboard when the outer office door opened.

The first thing she saw was a small, fat paw wrapped around the handle of a scuffed and over full, satchel type briefcase. It was followed by an arm attached to Dr. Rouard in a brindle brown suit towing his mistress, Estelle, along behind him. Estelle was her usual self, overflowing her dress wherever possible, bulging where not.

"Good morning Doctor," Beverly said from behind the safety of her desk. And since Rouard didn't look at her, she greeted Estelle with a distasteful look wrapped in silence.

"Isn't he here yet?" Rouard asked.

"Yes sir. Half an hour ago," Beverly replied.

Rouard looked shocked, turned to his inner office door. "You let him in my office?"

"No sir. He waited out here ten minutes, said he couldn't stand the computer noise and went in anyway."

Rouard scowled at the closed door while Beverly cringed. "Should I bring in some tea?" she asked meekly.

"No. It's going to be brief." He turned to his companion.

"Sit down my dear. I won't be long," he said, patting Estelle on the arm as she smiled back at him, then reached for the door knob.

He entered the violated space of his private office that contained his immense desk, too many chairs, a couple of bookcases, a large globe on a floor stand and the overflow from the outer office that clogged the remaining corridors. He found Sam Gorhman standing by the window, looking out. Rouard glared at the man, proceeded to the window and looked out too.

"Damned miserable city," he said. "Look at it, half under water."

Silence.

He turned to Sam. "Well, Mr. Gorhman. What brings you to New York?"

"Kinda between planes. Thought I might drop in."

Rouard took an exaggerated look at his watch. "How can I help you this time?"

"Being punctual might be a place to start," Sam said, giving him enough of a smile to be confusing.

"I beg your pardon?"

"You said ten thirty."

"I have a heavy schedule."

Sam moved around the desk to a chair. "Partying again last night?" he asked and sat down, not looking at Rouard.

Rouard gazed at the man, had to grant him innocence in asking the question and sat down in his own high backed chair.

"Any recent developments the public should know about?" Sam asked, thinking of the assignment he was supposed to be on.

"In what regard?"

"Have those billion dollar ground reflectors been of any value?"

"We seem to have verifiable evidence that they are working."

"You *seem* to have?"

"The earth's ecosystem is a very complex mechanism sustained in part by an atmospheric body of gases that is very dynamic, constantly changing and very difficult to assess."

"I took college physics too, remember? Before I became a journalist."

"Which is why I don't understand the question."

"Dammit, Doctor. We've already lost a sixth of the worlds population to ozone and greenhouse effects. Now you're gambling the fate of the rest of the human race on those

22

reflectors. You know that's a big damn joke."

"What? Excuse me. They are working exactly as predicted, reflecting sunlight back out into space to reduce global temperature. Besides, they've only been in place for two years."

"And?"

"A slight cooling trend may be in progress."

"Come on, Doctor. You know that's not true. Even if we could afford to put down a million square miles of them, the effect would still only be comparable to removing a few pails of water from the entire ocean."

"But they do work. At least I have proved that."

"Right! And so what? It's still valueless. What else have you come up with that might do some real good? I need something positive to take back to my editor."

"We have other research programs under way that look very promising."

"Such as what?"

"We're not prepared to share them with the public just yet but I assure you we are doing our very best to slow this thing down and turn it around."

"Well, that's really encouraging but how about something a little more specific. What about the ozone layer?"

After having heard the alarming news from Doctor Cairns in Australia last evening, the question caught Rouard a bit off guard. But surely there was no way this reporter could have known about it so he recovered quickly with the inane answer that the ozone layer was still largely intact.

"Jesus, you're impossible," Sam said, having caught the look on Rouard's face which betrayed him.

"Must you be so course?"

"I understand skin cancer is up three hundred percent from a year ago in some parts of the world. How do you account for that?"

"I'm not familiar with the statistics."

"No, I suppose not. Those statistics happen to be people."

"I doubt if they will all die."

"Your concern is overwhelming."

"We all know the population has to stabilize itself at some more sensible level. It's still too high for present conditions."

"Well, there I agree with you. And if we had spent some of those mega dollars on birth control instead of ground reflectors we might already be seeing some measurable progress."

"But you know that is still politically impossible, even with things as bad as they are."

"Unfortunately, I do. And it all comes back to religion. The pro-lifers think it is more humane to bring children into the world and let them starve to death or die of disease than it is to short circuit the process before hand. Then we have those other crazies who think that the only way the world will be saved is for them to out breed those with a different view of things, issues which gutless politicians are afraid to engage. What do you think?"

"Well said, I believe. So what other choice do we have for now but to let nature take its course until the population stabilizes at a more sustainable level?"

"I don't know. But we can't just give up. That's where you come in. You and your organization and all that money you have available and I don't see anything very specific or very promising in process."

"Perhaps not. But just between you and me, I can assure that I am working on something vastly important that will put the whole situation in a completely new perspective."

"Something I can quote you on, right?"

"Definitely not. I will deny that I have even spoken to you."

"Never mind. The public wouldn't believe it anyway."

A sheet of silence divided the two men. Rouard fidgeted in his chair, turned a page on his desk calendar. "Anything else?" he asked finally.

"What other countries are monitoring ozone depletion and rare gas concentrations besides the US.?"

"Brazil and South Africa. That's about it."

Sam rose nonchalantly from his chair, stretched, meandered over to the large floor globe, turned it slowly, stopped at Australia.

"I thought the Australians were the leaders in that field?" he asked casually.

"They are not a direct part of the United Nations scientific body."

"That Australian scientist, Doctor Carns..."

"Kairns, I believe is correct."

"Kairns. Do you suppose she's still doing atmospheric research?"

"That is quite possible."

"Any idea how I might be able to reach her?"

"Why would you want to do that?"

"Oh, I don't know. Sometimes it's nice to have a second opinion about things."

"I doubt if she would like to be bothered. I suspect that she's rather busy like the rest of us," Rouard said arrogantly, trying to dissuade Sam.

Convinced that he had indeed overheard something important the previous evening, Sam continued to push, however, but Rouard stood firm. No problem, Sam thought. He was finally beginning to enjoy what he had originally thought would be a very boring assignment. Unfortunately, he was still a long way from having anything worth printing. So, what next, he wondered, trying to remember how long it had been since he had last visited Australia and where he might find the lady scientist Rouard was so intent on shielding.

SIX

Seven hundred and twenty eight tons of gargantuan, throbbing, turbocharged diesel electric engines in tandem lumbered down the tracks at nearly one hundred kilometers per hour, dragging another six hundred thousand tons of squeaking, rattling, clanging, clicking and clacking cars and cargo behind. A hundred and sixty feet of engines, three quarters of a mile of flat cars, box cars, and coal cars on behind, all full.

Inside the cab the engineer tapped on the face of the

number two voltmeter, decided it was correct and slid back in his seat. He reached inside the coarse cloth of his work jacket, removed an oversized flask, unscrewed the cap, took a slug. Raw vodka flowed over diseased, nicotine stained teeth, across anesthetized taste buds and down a red, raw throat, hitting the already aggravated bottom of his stomach. Tissue cringed as the man patted his stout belly, grunted and felt warm again. Like a clock, one slug every fifty kilometers. Four more slugs to Liska, seven additional ones to Kiev. If the vodka held out and the stomach didn't spring a leak, he'd be home by sundown.

Politely he held the flask out towards the brakeman. Politely the brakeman did his usual refusal. He didn't need it. He was much younger and he was thinking of Kira, full and warm, waiting for him. Come on goddamned old train. Keep sucking up that diesel, turn them generators, keep them traction motors flowing with electricals, Kira's gonna get laid tonight. Quarter liter of vodka an hour for the engineer, sixteen hundred liters of diesel for the engines, sweet thoughts of a handsome young Russian girl for the brakeman. Come on baby, keep on rolling.

The brakeman leaned back, too, busy with his own private daydream as a small thump occurred on the front of the train, barely noticeable except for the sudden swirl of something over the side windows of the cab. The brakeman came alert, slid open the window, leaned out, looked down the track in front as railroad ties disappeared under the lead engine with a blur of graveled roadbed alongside. What's that, way down the track? Looks like a house high stack of hay on the tracks. He shouted to the engineer. The engineer managed to open his window. What the hell is this? Whoof, pow, more course, dry hay flew through the air.

Hurriedly, he brushed off his face, spit the dust out of his mouth, sneaked a quick second look out the window, then back out for another. Son-of-a-bitch, he said in his native tongue as he jerked back inside and reached for the controls. Air brakes first, actuators second. Iron on iron, grinding, squealing, growing red hot under the pressure, the resistor grid connected to the electric traction motors warming steadily, the train stretching out, slowing, slowing.

The brakeman was concerned. Would they stop in time? I hope to mother Russia that we do. They did. Barely. The third and largest haystack was a mere twenty feet away from the iron prow of the beast out front. A bigger, wider, taller haystack and this son-of-a-bitch was on fire. What the hell was going on? What were all those trucks coming out of the woods for?

Hassaan, skin the color and texture of old brown shoes, turban wrapped dark hair, eyes black and empty as the night, watched the action through binoculars from the fringe of the woods all green and heavy with the bursting buds of spring. By his side a mercenary in camouflage fatigues stood ready, a rocket launcher aimed at the last car of the train. Hassaan tapped him on the shoulder. A burst of flame exited the rear of the launcher tube as the ten centimeter projectile exited the front, speeding rapidly and impartially towards the target, hitting it dead center, instantly killing the twenty man squad of federal troops starting to disembark.

The first truck reached the engine. Soldiers with automatic weapons commanded the engineer and fireman to climb down. The soldiers climbed aboard and smashed the radio. Other trucks rolled up alongside certain boxcars. Staccato bursts of weapon's fire tore the padlocks off the doors, strong hands rolled them open. Weapons, ammunition, sacks of grain, canned goods and food supplies were off loaded and placed on the trucks. Twenty minutes later the trucks were rolling again, back into the protection of the woods. The guerrilla captain, a wild eyed, deviate of a man commanded his jeep driver to pull up alongside the engine.

"Comrades," he said to the engineer and brakeman as he stepped out of the vehicle and approached them. "You may return to the shelter of the engine but do not attempt to leave before three hours have passed." He pointed towards the woods at the soldier with the rocket launcher in readiness on his shoulder. "Do you understand?"

Hearty acknowledgment was expressed.

"Good," said the captain. "The hay pile will have burned down by then and it will still get you off the track before the next train. Have a safe trip, my friends."

"That son-of-a-bitch ain't no friend of mine," said the engineer as the jeep drove off, thinking that he would now run out of vodka. Bad enough to be going home to a cold house and a cold woman, but to have to arrive sober, dear god, it was asking too much.

"Nor mine. Or comrade either," replied the brakeman, thinking of his sweet, soft, Kira. Now it would be well after midnight before he could crawl in under those sheets. Thinking of her made it suddenly difficult for him to walk again. He let the engineer proceed up the steps into the cab ahead of him.

The soldiers retreated back into the woods from whence they came. The captain stopped to speak with Hassaan, nearly invisible now in the fast fading last light of the day. "A very nice haul, if I might say so, Sir."

"Yes. Soon your forces will have enough food and weapons to begin the move on Moscow."

It would be only minutes now until total darkness. By morning they would have disappeared entirely.

SEVEN

Outback Australia wasn't exactly the American southwest but it did have its own harsh kind of beauty, Sam thought as he sat gazing out the window of the old single engined Norman aircraft as it labored westerly five thousand feet above the hot, cinder dry landscape, sparsely scattered with touches of green.

"Pretty barren down there," Sam said to the pilot of the small craft.

"Looks a bit thin all right but it's still home to kangaroos, camels, wild horses and aborigines. Poor buggers. They're dying like flies anymore, what with the atmosphere deteriorating like it is."

"The aborigines?"

28

"All of them. The animals, too, but especially the aborigines. That's Ayers Rock there up ahead. One of their holy places."

"Yes, I climbed it once a few years ago."

"World's largest monolith," the pilot said proudly. "Course it's not as impressive as your American mountains but it's still a pretty big rock."

"Have you been to the States?" Sam asked.

The pilot took the plane almost directly over the huge red rock, banked slightly and headed northward in the direction of the Olgas. "No," he said after he was again on a straight course. "Only through books and movies."

"Well, I hope you make it someday."

"Me too, mate. I want to see some of that Edward Abbey country. Now there was a guy who could tell a story."

Sam was astounded. To think that he had come half way around the world only to met someone who also liked his favorite author. Some coincidence. "You've read his books?"

"Every one of them. Wish he'd lived to write some more."

"Me too. Which one did you like the best?"

"I'd say 'The Monkey Wrench Gang' probably."

"It was a classic, all right."

"You liked him too?"

"I guess if I ever had a hero when I was growing up, it was him," Sam said. "There was a time there when I was seriously contemplating blowing up Glen Canyon Dam myself."

"Well, if you decide to take it on, let me know. I'll come and help," the pilot said.

"Might just do that," Sam said, half seriously, as he began thinking of Abbey's reactionary attitude towards governmental control and big business manipulation. Perhaps if more people had shared his concern for the environment back then, things might be considerably different today. Unfortunately, at the time, people were much more willing to run off and slaughter their fellow man in the interest of oil and ethnic cleansing than they were in learning how to treat the planet with minimal respect.

"Let me know," the pilot said as he picked up the mike and called the airstrip at Alice Springs where they would be touching down in another minute.

Just two hours northwest of Alice Springs by auto beyond the end of the rust red road, two insane people rode in a battered old Land Rover as it roared across the desert floor, a rooster tail of red dust rising behind. The canvas half-top of the vehicle shaded the slightly more sane driver, protecting him from the dreaded ultraviolet of the sun. Michael, the man standing in the rear however, had to rely on his clothes, his wide brimmed hat, bandito scarf and male bravado to save his macho ass. The bucking, bouncing, four wheeled buckaroo was hard to hang on to. Especially when you were standing up in the rear holding onto an automatic rifle.

"Yaahooo," shouted Michael as the straining vehicle came up along side a tail thumping, running like all hell, confused by the noise, frightened to death, gaunt looking kangaroo.

Accompanied by another, YAAHOO, a rapid burst of fire emanated from the weapon and brought the indigenous creature down with a hard thump and a roll. Sad, questioning eyes looked at it's fleeing, unfeeling attackers who were already in search of a new target as the animal's red, life sustaining blood, redder even than the rocks and sand, seeped into the soil from a dozen fatal wounds.

Too far away, the shots went unheard and the slaughter unnoticed back at the mobile research camp which lay at the end of the dirt road cooking in the late afternoon sun, the dim echoes of rifle fire washed away by the sound of a petrol powered generator purring away behind the furthest trailer. Still penetratingly hot and deadly, the slanting sunlight reflected off the sand, the rocks and the rooftops of the vehicles where their occupants continued with their tasks while the sun drifted lower in the sky. Finally the door of the main trailer opened. Jill and Ernie stepped out into the approaching light of evening, walked a short ways to the crest of a low hill and sat down on a smooth, flat slab of sandstone and faced the dying sun.

"God, it's awful not to be able to feel the sun on your skin except early in the morning or just before sunset," Jill remarked, her long hair glowing in the light, more golden now than ever.

"Tragic that our benefactor, the giver of life, is turning into our enemy," Ernie replied.

"The sun hasn't changed," Jill said. "We're the ones who fucked it up."

That was another thing Ernie liked about his boss. Plain spoken and to the point. "And to think our parents used to worry about nuclear weapons," he said.

Silently they watched the sinking orb slide below the rim of their world, their unshared, private thoughts suddenly interrupted by the sound of a vehicle. Another Land Rover, newer and rented, rambled down the road and over the ruts. It headed towards the main trailer. They stood up. The driver saw them and turned their way, stopping nearby. Who the hell was this guy in the loose fitting clothing and a pith helmet? they both wondered. A pith helmet? Good god, where did he find that? Ernie asked himself. He hadn't seen one in years.

The man exited the machine and came closer, removing the thing from his head.

"You must be Dr. Kairns," Sam said, looking steadily at her, unwavering. There was no Ernie in the picture for him as yet, no desert, no sunset. There was only the blond goddess before him. He could see nothing else.

Somehow it didn't work, however. She tacitly refused to fulfill the dream that her presence evoked in him and quickly handed him off to Ernie. Ernie would give him a tour of the facility and answer his questions, she decided. Ernie wasn't too enthralled with the task, either, but he did it because he was a very decent chap. He was also proud of his association with Dr. Kairns and loved to speak of their work together. Except for "that" which they had discovered last week. That we won't talk about. Not yet anyway.

Half a world away the forbidden matter was the subject of

a different discussion. "It's absurd to say that the ozone depletion rate has gone nonlinear," said Dr. Rouard from behind his desk. "The theoretical model has been verified a hundred times."

"With all due respects Doctor Rouard," replied Dr. Korsak Kolowski, transplanted Russian scientist and Vice Chairman of UNAAC from his less desirable position in front of the desk as he held up a thick, bound sheaf of papers for emphasis. "I'm not one to argue with the facts."

"I won't accept raw data that hasn't been confirmed."

"She's the best there is in her field."

"And her field is not our main concern. Our concern is with the greenhouse effect and that's what we should be attending to."

"And the Dalheim research shows they are at least third order related. Neither is self limiting and ozone depletion is nearing logarithmic decay. And that's not even the serious part of it."

"So?"

"So I think we should have an emergency meeting of the full council and give Dr. Kairns a chance to present her findings."

"All in good time, my dear fellow."

"We are fresh out of time. Why are you stalling?"

"Need I remind you that I am the founder of this organization. You have only been Vice Chairman for a few months."

Dear God of Mother Russia, Korsak said to himself. This arrogant, bellicose bastard of a Frenchman has absolutely turned inside out. He was using his asshole for a mouth. And he doesn't want to discuss the technical possibility that his aging theoretical creation may have a few worm holes in it. Worse, using it to try and describe what's going on in the world today is like trying to match the shadow of a gorilla on the wall up with the shadow of an ostrich. And Rouard has turned into the ostrich. All body, no brain and head buried in the sand to boot. Somebody should drown him in the East River effluent. Let him choke to death on the solids in the sewage, that would be a fitting end.

Back in Australia, Ernie and Sam climbed the steps of the main trailer in the dim light of the small lamp wired to the top of a pole over the door. It was much cooler now and the door was open, welcoming the night air. Sam wondered if Jill was still inside. She was. He relaxed.

"Thank you for the tour," he said, offering Ernie his hand. "It was very interesting."

Ernie took the hand, shook it vigorously. Not a bad gent, this one, for an American anyway. Right to the point, all right.

"My pleasure mate," he said. "Would you like some tea?"

"No, just a chance to speak to Dr. Kairns before I leave. Thanks anyway."

Ernie hesitated, knowing she would object. But what the heck, he decided. Might do her good. Can't stand that other obnoxious dick brain who keeps hanging around.

"Of course," he said. "I'll call me wife. She'll be waiting."

"I hate to be so blunt Doctor, but I believe you are evading the issue," Sam said to Jill, even though it wasn't what he wanted to say. What he wanted to say was, who are you, what are you all about, how come you're so damned beautiful. No, it wasn't what he wanted to say at all, but, since she had evaded all his efforts at small talk, it was what came out of his mouth

"And I believe I have the right to do that sometimes."

"Why, for god's sake?"

"It's been my experience that the media is not to be trusted with a situation that's a bit too complex for the average layman."

"What's so damned complex about dying?" Sam asked sardonically.

"I don't know. Why, are you an expert in that field too?" she threw back at him, her intense blue eyes unblinking.

"Unfortunately, it's one of the things that goes with the territory."

Jill stared at him. "Gorhman. That's an unusual name."

33

Then the history of it came together in her mind. "Were you perhaps the one...?"

He gave her a confirming shrug and Jill was silent. There was a modest change for the better in her expression. She looked up at the wall clock. "I'm sorry to cut you short but I have other things to attend to," she said.

Sam didn't want to let her off the hook quite that easily, however, knowing that there was more of a story here than she was willing to talk about. His mind went back to Rouard. "Nonlinear?" the man had questioned when he had spoken to Jill on the phone that night at the party. He was sure of it. Nonlinear what?

Not pollution levels. They had to be falling with so many fewer people in the world. No, it had to be the ozone layer or some other degrading atmospheric phenomenon. But how and why? And if it was changing in some nonlinear way, why make such a big secret of it? Why all the hostility?

"Well, if you don't share your opinions with the media", he said. "Do you at least exchange information with other scientific groups?"

"Many of them."

"How about U N A C C?"

"When it's been appropriate."

"Recently?"

No answer. They stared at each other in equally formidable fashion, neither about to yield. Damn, Sam thought, secretly pleased. This was some lady, all right. They never got a chance to play it out, however, because the silence was soon interrupted by the disturbing engine noises of a loud vehicle outside. Jill grimaced at the sound of brakes and large, off road tires sliding in the gravel. The engine stopped. She looked subdued and somewhat embarrassed at the clomp of boots on the steps as Michael, the ignoble kangaroo hunter, entered the room carrying his automatic weapon. He leaned it against the wall and grinned voraciously at her through the film of dust on his face.

"Couldn't you at least leave that outside?" she said caustically.

"Sorry, babe. I forgot." He stared at Sam.

"And I told you not to call me that," she said, about to say more. But she dismissed it and introduced the two men instead.

"Mister, is it?" Michael said. "Not another scientist I take it?"

"Hardly. I'm a reporter."

"And a Yankee too. Are you a sportsman?"

"Michael...Please!" said Jill.

"Kangaroo hunting is great sport. Make a good story."

"You hunt kangaroo with that?"

"Sure mate. From the back of a Rover."

"Where the hell's the sport in that?"

"Poor bloody buggers are all gonna die anyway."

"And your an eschatologist practicing your own private brand of euthanasia. That's considerate."

Michael didn't understand specifically what he'd been called but knew he had been called something he knew he wouldn't like if he did understand it. He bristled. Sam stared back, challenging him to continue.

"Michael, please wait outside? I'll be able to talk to you in a minute."

Michael's eyes were cold and a bit wary. Who was this guy? He'd never been rebuked so openly before. And why was Jill being so hostile. She had never been that vehement with him before. He thought they were friends. Or, almost friends anyway. Somehow he didn't like it one bit. He picked up the rifle, took one last stab at preserving himself.

"Sure you're not a scientist? Sound like two of a kind to me."

Sam watched Jill's face as her eyes followed the swaggering figure out the door, trying to determine what unlikely connection there might be between the two of them, but there was no clue. And was that jealousy he had heard in the man's voice? Surely she couldn't be involved with such a sadistic misfit as this! Good god. Had he completely misjudged her?

"Seems like he has a bit of a problem," Sam stated after

he was gone but Jill refused to clarify the situation and remained silent. None of his business, right? Of course not, Sam told himself as he surveyed her delicate features. A mute, tightly controlled expression if he ever saw one, which revealed little in answer to any of his questions.

Jill, however, hoped her embarrassment didn't show. Whatever happened, she certainly didn't want to open things up to a discussion of her personal life. Not that she had one anymore, and certainly not with someone as gross as Michael. But it was still her business, not to be shared with some story hungry reporter. And this one, he might be hard to resist, if it came to that. He was attracted to her too, that part was clear enough. But for the time being, they were worlds apart. Best to keep it that way. She repeated her earlier statement about other matters needing attention, rose and extended her hand.

He took it, shook, lingered discretely and let it go, studying her eyes as he did so.

"Thank you for your time, Miss Kairns," he said, avoiding her professional title on purpose, letting her know he considered her scientific background secondary to her femininity. Ten other women only half so pretty might have been offended but she was secretly flattered and smiled at him at last, wishing she could be more open in her discussion of her work. He got up and headed for the door, his mind full of unanswered questions. He had a pretty good idea of what she had discovered but why the secrecy? What additional effect would it have on the world's population? And, most importantly from his own personal standpoint, would he ever get to see this woman again?

EIGHT

The starlight scope can be a very useful invention, both for spying on your girlfriend when she's off in the bushes with another man on a dark night, or for war. Collect a few photons from the desired scene with a lens, image them onto a photocathode surface, suck off the emitted electrons with a high voltage field, amplify them a few thousand fold, slap them up against a phosphorescent screen and you have a bright, clear picture that would otherwise be so dark a man couldn't be sure he wasn't pissing on his own boots.

The scene this time, however, was not a girl in the bushes or a man pissing. Instead, it was armed guards walking the perimeter of a high, barbed wire topped, chain link enclosure in the dim light of the moon sliver as seen from behind various porphyritic protrusions in the central Argentinean highlands. Inside the fence were block long rows of glassed roof buildings with acres of greenhouses reflecting the sparse light, helping dimly to further illuminate the men assigned to protecting them. Five guards in all, rifles slung over their shoulders, patrolled the area, each a clear and distinct target under the crosshairs of the starlight scope fitted rifles trained on them.

In even greater jeopardy was a barracks at the end, dead center in the sights of a familiar looking rocket launcher. A familiar brown skinned hand from one part of the world touched the shoulder of another brown skinned man from a different part of the world. Unrelated except in cause, they were for the moment a team and the Argentinean Indian responded by squeezing the trigger of the weapon.

A trail of whistling fire in the night caused the bunkhouse to instantaneously disappear as five other, sixty two gram slugs of steel jacketed lead hurtled through the exploding darkness and equated themselves with the unmatched softness of tissue and bone of the guards. Total elapsed time? One blink, or was it two?

Hassaan watched. Even he was impressed. So was the Jeffe, smiling in the dark. He turned on his flashlight, signaling. The roar of starting engines replaced the sounds of the brief massacre. A circle of headlights came on out by the periphery of the complex. Gears clashed. The waiting trucks began to converge over the rough terrain, avoiding the vantage point rocks and boulders used by the assaulting snipers. Behind the trucks a hoard of people raised their voices in a victory shout and followed them through the now crumbled fences and into the compound. The Jeffe's chest swelled even more. Something for the people, that's what it was all about. Something for the people, food for the poor starving people. Cause enough. Who cares what the motives of the foreigner were.

"Not a single casualty," he said proudly.

"The Argentinean National Army will soon be too hungry to fight," said Hassaan.

"So, when can we expect the medium range surface to surface missiles?"

"When you have proved yourself ready for the final offensive on Buenos Aires."

"And after that, will we attack Brazil?"

NINE

"It's snowing, for christsake," said the crackly voice coming from somewhere inside the scraggly looking middle aged woman in an old print dress that was faded so badly that the floral design looked like dried food stains instead of patterns.

"I can see," said the old man in line in front of her, readjusting a battered old felt hat on his head.

"Yeah, but it's July, dammit. Don't you know that?"

"Of course I know it. My birthday was just last week."

"But this is Chicago! It doesn't snow in Chicago in July. It's summertime."

"Well, maybe you're hallucinating or something," said the bleary eyed old man, brushing flakes off his tender looking, red bulb of a nose.

"It's the Russians, damn them. They're doing it."

"Jesus lady," said a better dressed, middle aged man, one place closer to the door. "We've been friends with the Russians for over ten years. It's the Chinese."

"And you're a fool," said the woman. "That's exactly what they want us to think. Until they can find a better way to harass us."

"It's our lack of spirituality," put in the stringy haired, moon faced young woman next in line who hid her immensely

38

dilated eyeballs behind a pair of grannie shaped, purple sunglasses. "We all need to work a little harder at increasing our vibrational attunement to higher frequencies so we can transmute all the negative energies out of the astral planes."

"Transmute, my ass," said the first woman, just as the door of the market burst open and an unshaven younger man was forcefully evicted from the building.

He shook himself free from the burly guard, turned and yelled.

"Sons a bitches," he said. "Rotten meat, no fruit and no vegetables. What the hell do we need ration coupons for?"

"Get outa here," said the guard.

"Fuck you, asshole," the young man said and walked off.

The door opened again, more slowly this time, as Jean walked out carrying two small bags of groceries. She was despondent. God, she thought. What a hell of a way to live, standing in line, pawing over barely edible food, cramped into an undersized apartment with her parents. No personal freedom, no private life, no fresh air or open land, no trees and what was beginning to look like, no work for Bud. How much longer could they hold out?

She shuffled along, huddled against the bizarre, unseasonable cold, not really looking where she was going, not really caring either, moving closer to a narrow, dark, endless looking alley, unaware of the two young hoodlums who waited around the corner. The tall one slammed into her as she came abreast of their hiding place and knocked her down while the younger one grabbed the two sacks and fled back down the alley followed by his companion.

"I'm sorry, honey," Bud said. "It's my fault. I should have come with you."

"No Bud. It's not. It's this damned city," Jean said angrily as she plunked herself down on the old couch. "We don't belong here and we shouldn't have come in the first place."

"But what about...them? Your father?"

Jean caught a glimpse of movement in the hall and gave Bud a look just as her mother came into the room. Still petite and full of patience, the older woman asked, "did you find what you needed at the store, dear?"

"Part of it. But I never made it home."

"What happened?"

"I guess you could say I was mugged. The little bastards caught me by surprise."

"Now dear, you mustn't swear like that. You know father doesn't approve."

"Well, I should have known better. I was raised in this neighborhood, remember?"

"Yes, and I have to admit, you were quite able to take care of yourself back in those days, all right," her mother said proudly. "Why, remember the time that boy up the street..."

"Mother, please. I don't think Bud is interested in my adolescence."

Bud sat down beside her and put his arm around her. "Who says I'm not?" he teased. "Please finish what you were going to say, Mrs. Redfeather."

"Don't you dare, mother."

"Well, maybe some other time," Jean's mother said and smiled at Bud. "Right now I'd better get your father his medicine."

"Daddy's home?"

"Yes. While you were at the store. He wasn't feeling so good again."

Jean rose and went the short distance down the hall. A moment later she was back. "I think he's sleeping," she said.

"Why don't we go for a walk," Bud proposed. "Maybe we can find another store that's open."

"Supper will be at six," Jean's mother informed them.

"God, I don't know how they can go on living here," Jean said as they stepped over the trash and rubble on the sidewalk.

"Habit, I suppose. They probably don't even see it anymore. At least not the way we do."

"I miss the farm so much, Bud. I wish we could have stayed. It was the best part of my life."

"Mine, too. But mostly because you were there."

40

"Someday, maybe we can go back and see it again."

"And make love under the willow tree?"

"I hope so. I love you so much, Bud. And it was nice to have all that freedom. To be able to shout if I wanted. To feel the sun and the rain on my face. To be able to pull my pants down and have you in me any time I wanted."

"Except for that time in the barn when Jenkins drove up. It's a good thing he thought you were screaming at the cows."

"And here we are, sharing this mouse hole with my parents. The bed squeaks and the walls are so thin we can't even talk."

Bud stopped and turned her towards him. He put his hands on her shoulders.

"As soon as I find a job, maybe we could get a hotel room for a night or two."

"Why don't we just move?"

"Where to?"

Jean was silent for a moment. "Do you think the car would get us to California?" she asked at last.

"It might, if no one steals anymore parts off it. But, why there? It's a long ways from Chicago."

"Because we'd be happier there. I'm sure you could find work. What about that hydroponics station you had an offer from last year?"

"What about your parents? Do you think they would come?"

"Mother might. But not as long as dad is still alive. And you know him. Stubborn as his arthritis and just as inflexible. This is where he will die. And not so far off, by the looks of him."

"Maybe we should stay a while longer. We have money left."

"No we shouldn't. I have already had that discussion with mother. She doesn't want it that way. If there was work and we stood some chance of being happy here, it might be different but she would never feel right about it if we were just hanging around making a sacrifice."

Bud considered her words. "Well, maybe we can send

them some money once we get settled. It might make it a little easier."

TEN

Sam sat at his desk surrounded by the clutter of journalism. Papers, scraps of paper, reports, computer printouts, notepads, a well thumbed dictionary, a brown stained coffee cup, various mementos and memorabilia, photos pinned to the walls and a large world map opposite his desk liberally sprinkled with little red headed map pins covering the continents, denoting the wide scope of his travels. He was on the phone listening, watching a small black ant walk head down across the glowing face of his computer screen, stop at the disk slot and peer in, its long feelers wiggling briskly, sampling the air in front of it.

"Don't go in there, you little shit," Sam said without thinking.

"What did you say?" asked the female voice on the phone.

"I was just talking to this little ant who was about to get himself eaten by my computer," Sam said. "Looks like he changed his mind, however. He's heading around to the back."

"What are you talking about?" came the laughing question from one of the research assistants in the company archives.

Before Sam could answer however, Cliff stalked into his office scowling, holding a few sheets of paper in his hand.

"Let me call you back in a bit," Sam said and hung up.

Cliff shook the papers in front of him. "What the hell is this supposed to be?" he demanded.

"I thought it was a story," Sam stated.

"Speculation, yes. A story, no. You can't attack Rouard like this. You make him out to be some kind of woolly old bandit."

"He is an old bandit, the son-of-a-bitch."

"I'm sorry you think so but we're not going to publish your distorted views of the man in this newspaper, no matter what."

"Give me a break, Cliff. I'm trying to shake something loose."

"Yes, my career if we print it. I want facts, not allegations."

"Oh shit," Sam said as he reached for the phone and punched two numbers. "Julie," he said, when it was answered. "Find out who the new Vice Chairman of UNACC is, get me an appointment with him, then book me a flight to New York."

"Dammit Sam," Cliff interrupted. "Did you ever think of using the phone to interview people? You're already twice over budget on your travel allowance."

Sam thought of using the phone all right, but not for anything serious. He had enough trouble getting at the truth when it was done face to face and eyeball to eyeball.

"And make it as soon as possible," he told Julie as Cliff's scowl deepened even further.

Korsak, the Cossack, or so he was called by nearly everyone except Dr. Rouard. A hearty, giant of a man who looked like he had been mistakenly born into the wrong era, yet a man who more than did justice to his place behind a desk. He was as intelligent as he was exuberant. Sam liked him immediately, although he earnestly wondered how such a man could tolerate a full time association with someone so disdainful as Rouard. Well, maybe someday they would get a chance to discuss it. For the moment, however, Sam had other questions in mind. He stuck to the amenities for a polite moment longer, then got more nearly to the point of his visit. Did Korsak know of Dr. Kairns?

"Now that is a good looking woman," Korsak said avidly. "Yes, I met her, I think it was three years ago at a world conference. Unfortunately at the time, she was married."

He sighed briefly at the thought, then continued. "And besides that, from a professional point of view, I'd have to have spent my career at the bottom of a frog pond not to be aware of her exceptional work in atmospheric studies."

Internally, Sam flinched. Why should he feel

43

uncomfortable knowing that Jill had been married? Maybe she had children and an ex husband who was still around. He hesitated, checking his curiosity. Besides, as much as he liked this man here, he wasn't going to ask a bunch of personal questions about the woman from someone who might have the same thing on his mind as he did. Then suddenly he felt flustered, thinking about how damned beautiful Dr. Kairns, Jill, really had been.

"Have you had an opportunity to meet her yourself?" Korsak asked.

Sam stated that he had recently been to Australia.

"Well then, you know what I'm talking about."

"I do. But what is her connection to Rouard?" Sam asked, not wanting to discuss something so personal with someone who was still a stranger.

"She is under contract with UNACC at the time being. This means she continues to monitor and study upper atmospheric effects and phenomenon and we get the results."

"Which means what? That she can't publish independently?"

"Unfortunately not without Dr. Rouard's personal approval."

"How did something like that happen?"

"The Australian government is on the verge of bankruptcy and she was out of funding."

"Do you think her research is important?"

"Very."

"You said it's concerned with the upper atmosphere. Have there been any recent dramatic changes in that area?" Sam asked as he watched Korsak's face carefully. "Say in the ozone layer, for example?"

Korsak may have blinked slightly but he hung onto his composure quite well.

"Why do you have an interest in that specific topic?" He asked as he looked at Sam, revealing nothing.

"Because it's one more thing that is of vital importance to our long range survival if it continues to deplete. And, what if, for example, the depletion rate went non linear? What then?"

44

"That would not be a good situation," Korsak finally said after staring back at Sam for a long moment, now realizing that here was a person he would have a hard time side stepping issues with and so, not knowing where to go from there, he said nothing.

Sam didn't say anything for a long moment either. Then he asked Korsak how long he had been in New York and had he ever been to one particular restaurant. And when Korsak said no, he asked if he would like to go. They could meet there that evening. And, since Sam had a female friend he could bring, what if he asked her to ask a friend along for Korsak since it was obvious that the Russian liked women. Whatever it took, Sam thought. Even though he was beginning to like the man, he was still determined to loosen him up and get some valid information to go home with.

The restaurant they met at was high and dry on the upper east side. It was the first time Sam had met Schalla's friend Lydia, a tall, dark haired woman who had recently decided she had been single long enough and needed a man to share some of the amenities of her life with, including the more than ample share of her divorce settlement. She was also very charming, as was Korsak who seemed pleased with his blind date. There was a healthy banter throughout dinner and on the surface it appeared that the match had been a good one. Korsak told vigorous tales of his Russian boyhood while Lydia laughed and gave him all her womanly signals of approval and receptivity, both verbally and physically and there was little doubt that the Cossack would have his hands full later on, if he chose to take advantage of it.

On the other hand, however, there was something else going on beneath the surface. Subtly and innocently enough in the beginning, the players were hardly even aware of it themselves, but it grew as their meal progressed. Half way through Sam began to pick up on it, although he was sure that by the time it had became apparent to him, Lydia's mind was already in her bedroom with Korsak.

Fascinated, Sam watched as Schalla and Korsak became

silently entangled, unaware of the direction they were headed in. Obviously they had been caught off guard themselves, each not sure of what the other was thinking at first, but, by the end of the main course they had to be realizing that it must be mutual. Secretly embarrassed by then, however, they discreetly worked very hard to steer things in a different direction. But Sam saw it and studied it and examined his own feelings in the matter while the intangible little lines of force pulled away, working their magic as the chemistry of it radiated invisibly back and forth across the table without a word being spoken. As for his own feelings, he was a bit bothered at first but then, seriously, even though Schalla was a very desirable woman, they were truthfully still just friends. Good friends to be sure but the kind of chemistry that would have been necessary to carry it over into a different realm was never really there. So, being realistic, beginning to like and respect Korsak, what else was there to say. It was Lidia's dream that would be shattered, not his. And even though it hadn't completely defined itself yet, his own unrealized dream was to be with someone else also.

Meantime, as the evening progressed, on the other side of things Korsak also cagily and subtlety checked Sam out, perhaps fooling the women in the process but Sam still knew what he was after. Could Korsak trust him and what might his motivation for digging so hard into what Dr. Kairns had discovered and what would he do with the information if he were told the truth? That learned, the evening was over. Korsak, being the gentleman that he was, called for a cab and would see that Lydia got home safely. The same for Sam and Schalla. And Sam, now having completely clarified his feelings about her, would be truthful and tell her how happy he was for her, knowing that they would still be the best of friends, no matter what.

ELEVEN

Two days later the two men had lunch together. Korsak had talked to Dr. Kairns and she had confirmed her findings to him, cautioning him on Dr. Rouard's position about any disclosure as yet. Despite that, Korsak had indicated to Sam that his suspicions were correct, although he didn't elaborate on the extent of the problem.

"Damn," Sam said. "The story has to come out, you know that."

"Unfortunately, it does. But it would be nice if we could get some approval first. Hopefully from Rouard so the old goat doesn't go ballistic. But especially from Dr. Kairns, since it is her work."

"I understand," Sam said, thinking about the dilemma. So far all he really had was a headline with few actual facts to back it up. So, he could go with that and hope that put enough pressure on Rouard to come forward with the rest of the story, or, wait and hope Dr. Kairns would think of the bigger picture, defy Rouard and give the information to the press herself. Hopefully, to him specifically. As for asking Korsak to betray Jill and Rouard both, yes, he could do that. But he wasn't about to. Not yet at any rate. There had to be a better way so he shrugged and said it probably wouldn't hurt to wait a few more days. Perhaps Rouard would come to his senses.

"Fair enough," Korsak stated. "And there is also one more reason why that might be best. Dr. Kairns told me she is talking with NASA and would like them to relocate one of their satellites to the southern hemisphere."

"Of course," Sam stated, immediately realizing exactly why. "That would help confirm everything, wouldn't it?"

"What?"

"Long wavelength infrared spectrophotometer data. I understand there are still two of those satellites in operation. So, if the ultraviolet radiation reaching the earth's surface is already affecting sea life, it has to be affecting plant life as well. Even though trees and plants may still look healthy visually, the long wavelength data would tell if they were in trouble days, weeks or sometimes months before."

Obviously impressed, Korsak asked Sam how he would know such a thing and was told that Sam had once been in the technical field, no elaboration given. And with that they again agreed to wait because if the problem was as bad as Sam suspected, NASA would release the information directly to the press, again hopefully to him as a reporter because that's whose door he would be pounding on next. Then, when they had finished eating, Sam handed Korsak a slip of paper.

"What's this?" Korsak asked in a puzzled voice.

"Schalla's home phone."

"But what am I supposed to do with it?"

"Call her."

A look of embarrassment crossed the Russian's broad face.

"My friend," said Sam. "It's not a problem. I'm not in love with her, but maybe you are. Check it out."

Korsak's face reddened even more and he looked uncomfortable.

"So, call her," Sam said. "I think she'd like to hear from you."

It was nearly noon two days later when Sam caught the elevator to the seventeenth floor. He was anxious to see Korsak again. Korsak had talked to Jill once more but she had strongly cautioned him again on Dr. Rouard's position. Additionally, and just as bad, Korsak had told Sam that there was some kind of problem getting satellite data from NASA. Why he didn't know but it became a point of interest as far as Sam was concerned. And what about Rouard? Had the Russian made any progress with him, Sam also wondered, as he got off the elevator.

By the time he found his way to Korsak's office however, the Russian was putting some of his personal effects into packing boxes, thereby creating a bit of a shock. But Korsak straightened up as Sam entered the room and gave him a broad grin.

"Ah, Sam," he said good naturedly and extended his hand.

"Looks like I caught you at a bad time."

"Not at all. Come in, come in."

"What's all this? Are you moving to a new office?"

"A short but brilliant career," Korsak stated instead, and laughed.

"What is that supposed to mean?"

"Since I am now completely convinced that Dr. Kairns' data is correct I confronted Rouard. He refused to inform the rest of the governing board so I threatened to do it for him and a meeting was held. He treated me rather crudely in front of the membership, so I told him to go stuff it, as you say here in America."

"But he can't fire you if my understanding of UNAAC is correct. Each nation has the right to appoint their own representatives."

"True, but he chose to remove me from the Vice Chairmanship."

"So what are you doing? Quiting?"

"Absolutely not. But there are also serious political problems back home in my own country. I have had no news from my family since the fighting began. This gives me a good opportunity to go see if I can find them."

"How much family do have?"

"My father and sister and a few cousins. Not so much anymore."

"How long will you be gone?"

"A few days, maybe a week. There is not much reason to stay longer. My sister is married and my father rarely recognizes anyone anymore, so, if everything is all right, I will come back."

"Good."

"Yes. Yes. Besides, now I have another reason also. Schalla and I both thank you for that."

"Good. We need you here."

Korsak picked up one of the smaller boxes and sat it near the door.

"That will be my homework while I'm gone," he said and went to his desk chair and sat down. He waved towards one of the other chairs.

The two men sat and looked at each for a moment. "Who do you think is responsible for the fighting in Russia?" Sam asked.

"Some say our own people, some say the Arabs."

"As in Argentina?"

"Yes, it is the same."

"What part of Russia are you from?"

"Saratov, near the Volga. Where the munitions train was stopped two weeks ago."

"Well, if I can wrap this story up, perhaps I can come and see you. That's the assignment I really want."

With that Korsak rummaged through one of his desk drawers and extracted a thick document held together with brass eyelets.

"Meanwhile, perhaps this will give you something to occupy your time," he said, handing it to Sam. I have tried to summarize the findings in the back."

Sam quickly flipped through the pages. "Dr. Kairns data?"

"Yes. But no satellite data. There won't be any."

"What happened?"

"Well, they were already in the desired polar orbits but the military has taken them over. Now any and all data they may produce requires a top secret clearance, need to know only."

"Seriously?"

Again Korsak opened a desk drawer and handed Sam a piece of paper. One that had come directly from the White House and was signed by someone named Morely whose title was Director, not saying what he was director of. Sam read it and his eyebrows went up. "Son-of-a-bitch," he said as he shook his head in disbelief and handed it back but Korsak indicated that he could keep it.

"What do you think?" Korsak asked. "Why would they want to do that?"

"I don't know but I'm beginning not to like it. Obviously Dr. Kairns' data is correct and maybe she really believes it shouldn't be released because the public wouldn't be able to handle it, but as for Rouard, I don't know. Seeing this letter tells me something else is involved. Something not good."

"I see what you mean but I still have the highest regard for Dr. Kairns. Rouard, on the other hand, I have never trusted. As to what you should do with the data now that you have it, I don't know for sure."

"Thank you, and don't worry. I won't tell anyone how I came by it."

"I respect that, but it doesn't matter about me. Use it as you see fit and let's hope Dr. Kairns comes to understand because mostly it belongs to the American people anyway "

"How so?"

"I believe they paid for it."

"What do you mean?"

"Why don't you ask Dr. Kairns? Maybe you need an excuse to talk to her some more."

"My editor would kill me if I flew back to Australia again."

"You don't have to. She's right down the hall."

"Here?"

"Who do you think got my old job?"

Sam waved the waiter off again. How was he ever going to have any serious conversation with this lady if that damned fool kept hovering over them all the time trying to keep his water glass full? He was having enough difficulty concentrating as it was. Surely, a silk blouse with buttons down the front had to be the sexiest thing ever invented, especially when the bra underneath allowed for a certain amount of bounce and jiggle with the barest of movement. Her face, however, was even more fascinating as he kept falling into the deep blue of her eyes.

"So who was that great and fearless kangaroo hunter who showed up at your outback camp when I was there?" he asked, knowing it might be risky to do so since he had no idea as to what kind of relationship she might have had with the man.

Jill looked back at him across the table of the plush booth they sat in. She reached for her wine glass.

"Just one of the local bullies I had the misfortune of befriending", she said with a shrug and took a sip of her

51

Cabernet. "He used to haul fresh water out to the camp for us when we first set up."

"Does he really kill animals with an automatic rifle?"

"I think I finally got him to stop. Your comment to him might have helped a little, too. Even though I'm sure he didn't understand a word of it."

"Let's hope so," Sam said, looking at her.

"Anyone else in your life?" he asked after a further moment.

"Just because I agreed to have dinner with you doesn't mean I approve of so many non-technical questions."

"Sorry," Sam said, suddenly feeling rather helpless. "I seem to have an overriding curiosity about things that intrigue me."

"Me?" she laughed. "I'm not even sure I like you."

"I might not like you either, after the curiosity wears off," Sam said, telling the biggest lie of his life.

"Fair enough."

"So, let's return to business. Tell me about Rouard. I sense the connection goes back a bit?"

"He was a friend of my fathers. They were both geophysical graduates of MIT."

"Is that why you became a scientist?"

"He arranged an American scholarship after my father died."

"Well, that explains the loyalty," Sam said off handedly.

She gave him a look. "But there's more on your mind than that. What's the rest of it?"

"Oh, I just wondered why you chose to hide the fact that you have obviously made some very important, and very serious discovery regarding atmospheric conditions and why you have all this reluctance to share your technical findings."

"Are you sure you're not making a lot of rash assumptions?"

"In my business you can never be sure of anything."

"So why do you do so much speculation?"

"In this case I don't think it's speculation. I think it's real but there seems to be some kind of conspiracy to cover it up,"

52

he said, regretting the accusation the moment the words left his mouth. Dammit. Why couldn't she just trust him. He had her cold anyway. Why couldn't she at least try and discuss it with him.

"Oh, you are so tough, aren't you?" she said.

"At least I don't withhold information from the public that I think they are entitled to."

"Sometimes the public isn't ready for certain information. What if it was really serious? The public might react in ways that were not in their own best interest."

"Sorry, but I happen to have a little more faith in them than that. That's the mistake every administration in this country has made in the last fifty years."

"But it's true!"

"No it isn't, dammit. If you hide the truth, they will only react to it more strongly when they learn of it. Worse, they will no longer trust you when you need their trust the most."

"Maybe there are extenuating circumstances."

"How could there be?"

"UNACC provides two thirds of the funding for the Australian Geophysical Institute. By agreement with my government, Dr. Rouard has first right to all the data."

"And the United States provides three fourths of the funding for UNACC, which in my book gives the American public the right to see it."

"You make it sound so simple."

"It is."

"Don't be so sure."

"What's that supposed to mean?"

She looked at her watch. "I think it means I had best be getting home. I still have a lot of unpacking to do. Maybe you can get me a taxi."

Sam asked her where she was staying and found it to be only a few blocks away. Wanting the extra time together, he proposed that he walk her to her apartment.

"I've been told that it's not safe to walk the streets here, especially after dark."

"I wouldn't recommend that you do it alone."

"Yes, but I was told it is much worse since the waterfront areas have been flooded. The gangs have increased and moved into other parts of the city."

"The gangs have been roaming the city for as long as I can remember. It's just that there are more of them now because of the economic recession and all the social dropouts."

"I'd feel safer in a taxi."

"Either way. But, I'd feel better if I saw you to your door," said Sam.

"Are the taxies not safe, either?"

"Not always."

"Well, let's walk then."

The street was unseemingly quiet for the still early hour. There had been a light shower while they were having dinner but now the sky was nearly clear again and the light of the half moon reflected off the puddles on the sidewalk.

"Why are so few of the street lights lit?" Jill asked.

"Energy conservation. Don't you think it's about time?"

"Yes, but they're still using incandescent bulbs."

"That's New York. So much money still goes in someone's pockets that they can't afford the newer, luminescent spheres."

"Are you serious?"

"Yes."

They walked along, sharing trivialities. Sam reached for her hand. She didn't object. Suddenly she started confiding in him about the general nature of her research and her findings.

"So all right," Sam said. "So you admit there's a serious problem. But what caused it and how do you reverse the effects before it's too late?"

"It may already be too late."

"It may have been too late fifty years ago. How does anyone know for sure?"

"We've always known what caused ozone depletion. Unfortunately we don't know why such a sudden, dramatic change for the worse. Since we haven't isolated the cause, or causes, we aren't in a position to make proposals about how to correct it."

"Am I wrong or is something else going on also?"

"We haven't been able to confirm it directly."

"What?"

She didn't reply.

"It must be really serious. What is it?"

"Only if I have your complete silence."

"Fair enough," Sam said.

"It looks as though those millions of tons of atmospheric CFC's and other pollutants are undergoing chemical changes in the tropopause."

"Isn't that normal?"

"Yes, but this is different."

"Meaning what?"

"Radical recombinations into highly toxic substances that are potentially harmful to all life forms."

"In what way?"

"One form is possibly genetically altering. Birth defects and all that. Another looks molecularely very similar to Sarin, which is a nerve gas, if you remember."

"What next?"

"We aren't sure. Thus far we don't have sufficient information to determine if these things have had any biological impact on the planet. Since nobody has looked, it's possible that some of the deaths are from these agents. We also don't know how wide spread they are, how stable, If the trend is building or decaying, if we have an antidote or if one is even possible."

"And all this is in addition to ozone depletion. That's what has gone nonlinear?"

"Yes. That too."

They walked in silence, unable to share their concerns any further, each haunted by the feeling that perhaps it was indeed too late for the earth in terms of the bigger picture. Unheard, an electric powered car rounded the corner behind them and came down the street with only the parking lights on.

In the dim light of the evening it strayed too close to the curb, splashing water up onto the sidewalk. Instinctively they moved back, getting in each others way. Sam put his hands on her arms, pulled her close and kissed her.

"I thought you didn't like me," she said.

"I never really said that, but even if I had, it still doesn't mean that I didn't want to kiss you."

"Strange logic. Is that typically American?"

"Who knows," he said, and kissed her again, longer this time. "What's your excuse?" he asked.

"Frankly I'm a bit horny at the moment," she replied. "But that doesn't mean I'm going to sleep with you, either. Now, or later. Do you understand? There has to be more to it than that."

"Agreed," Sam stated as they continued to walk.

Once they reached her apartment building they sat on the front steps and Sam shared some of the adventures of one of his African trips with her. As she listened, another part of her mind worked busily away in the background. How things had changed. There was such an urgency to everything anymore and so little time for personal indulgence, peace and intimacy. And now there was the additional responsibility of her new position. How could she keep it all from sucking her dry? She sighed and leaned back, looking up at the sky. Even in these times of forced energy conservation, the light pollution from the city was still so strong as to make everything but a few of the brighter stars invisible. Sam finished his story and she thanked him for it. A taxi went by, then a few cars and a kid on a bicycle. She reached over and touched his arm. "I'm still horny," she said.

And when it was over and she lay sleeping like a precious kitten beside him, Sam could only wonder what the morning would bring. What did she feel, how did she feel? Was he there only because she was horny? What if someone else had taken her to dinner instead of him? Who then would be sharing her bed? And what about the research? Was she willing to cross the line? How would she feel if he published the findings anyway? Could he do such a thing after tonight? Was that why he was really here? Was he trying to use her or was she trying to use him? And what about sleep? It would be nice to get some sleep, just a little. He snuggled closer to her warmth and shut his eyes.

She watched him intently as he did the last few buttons of his shirt and gave him a quick hint of a smile. Sam sat down on the edge of the bed and kissed her gently, then rose again and stuffed in his shirt tail.

"Can I call you later?" he asked.

"Thank you, Sam." she replied instead.

He turned to her with an uncomprehending look. She couldn't be thanking him for the sex, could she? That would be ridiculous.

"Not for that, dammit," she said clearly.

"I didn't think so, but what then?"

"For not asking me to give you a copy of my research."

"Did you think I might try and use you?"

"I wasn't sure. Would you?"

"Frankly, I don't know and fortunately I don't have to worry about it."

"But you want to publish the story. I know you do."

"Yes I do, and I probably will."

"How can you? I may have admitted that your speculations are true but I won't confirm them publicly nor will I give you any official documentation."

"I already have a copy."

A look of surprise and shock crossed her face, then a fleeting look of something else. What was it? Fear? But it was gone too soon to grasp with assurance, replaced by anger.

"Where did you get it?" she demanded.

"Don't ask."

"Sam! You can't. I won't let you."

"Dammit Jill, I have to."

"Why?"

"Because I'm aware of it."

57

"That's ridiculous."

"You know it's not."

"Then do it for me."

"Is that why you let me into your bed? In case something like this should come up?"

"Well, go to hell. How could you even say something like that?"

"Because I'm a reporter and you knew that when you went out with me. As well as what I've been digging for."

"You're right. But I can say the same to you? Is that the only reason you took me out? So you could get me in bed and hope that your manhood would get me to agree? Did you think it would be that easy?"

"Not at all. I would have been very disappointed if it were."

"What then? Did you just want to get laid? Are you happy now?"

'I was happy just being able to take you to dinner. You're the one who said she was horny."

"I did, didn't I. And I was, damnit. I haven't been in bed with a man for a long time and I was beginning to think it wasn't even important any longer."

"But?"

"But for some dumb reason I found you to be kind of sexy and if you don't mind, I'd like to leave it at that."

"I, ah, jeez Jill. I'm.."

"It's okay. You don't have to say anything. And right now I'd prefer that you didn't."

"Yeah. I... damn," Sam muttered. What a predicament. Yes, he was falling in love with her. Totally. And she knew it so why did they have to end up disagreeing about such an important issue? An extremely important issue. One where time could indeed be running out for the human race. If only scientists hadn't been so smug, self righteous and silent over the years, mother nature wouldn't be having such a bad time of it right now. If they had had the guts to stand up to the politicians, the entrepreneurs, the power hungry and speak out about what they knew and could foresee, the world might not be in the doomsday situation it was in today. So, what about Jill? Was she part of the same group? She was saying one thing, but did she really mean it? No, he decided, bottom line. It was just that she was in a very difficult situation politically and the kindest thing he could do was to leave her alone about it for the time being. Then he looked at her there, sitting up in bed, looking back at him.

"I'm still horny," she stated as she slide over a bit and patted the sheets beside her.

TWELVE

Jill's mind kept drifting away from the paperwork piled up in front of her. She was full of conflicting emotions and thoughts. Why did she have to feel everything so strongly? Why couldn't she just take everything in stride, one day at a time, like everyone else? What was going on? One minute she felt like laughing, one minute she wanted to cry and the next a flush of sensuality swept over her? She'd certainly like to live the night she had with Sam over again. And the morning too, that was for sure. She could still feel Sam's hands on her breasts, his body rhythm warm and deep inside. She squirmed in her seat.

Yes, she'd certainly do that with him again no matter what they might think of each other. And that was very decidedly a rare feeling indeed. It had been a long time since any man had evoked such arousal in her. And where was he now, when she felt this way? Probably back in Los Angeles, dammit, trying to create his fateful Armageddon story, in spite of her wishes. Well let him try.

She tried to visualize what his office might be like, what he might look like sitting at his desk. And what was Los Angeles like? Hot and smoggy probably, and pretty awful too, like New York, only worse after all that had happened to it. God, big cities were dreadful places, she thought and shuddered. Buildings that blocked out the sun and the sky, traffic that fouled the air with sound and stench, and the people, good god, the people, all the damned people. Spilling out of buildings, clogging the sidewalks, pushing and shoving, getting in each others way, hassling and hustling, clinging to their semi-existence with shuttered minds, still chasing dollars, denying their humanity and their god, depriving each other of their sanity and their love.

Poor things. Perhaps that's what happened when people lost communion and connection with nature. And now the world was full of generations of them who had lived their entire lives surrounded by brick, concrete and stucco without benefit of clear blue skies and white clouds, green grass and trees, bird songs, animals roaming wild, distant horizons. None of it. They knew none of it. Millions and millions of people the world over who knew little or none of it. Of mankind's dependency on, and connection to nature, the real truth of things.

Instead they pushed and shoved, beat on, beat up, betrayed. There was no peace, no solitude, no where to go to rejoice or to think clear thoughts or even to be alone except behind some triple locked door someplace. There was no unity with their fellow man, their planet or themselves. How could you expect them to even understand the problem? They didn't, even back when there was still time. And now it was too late, very nearly, too late.

Jill swiveled around in her chair and sat looking westward out at what she could see of the city skyline and started to cry. Why did she feel so helpless? Deep down she knew Sam was right about giving her findings to the public. People needed to know the truth, good or bad but for now she had to maintain some level of loyalty to Rouard if she was going to continue her work. But what was she doing here buried in administrative tasks? Why had she come? What did she really expect to accomplish working within the confines of such an organization as UNACC so subjected to outside political pressure and manipulation? And what had happened to Rouard himself? Why did he bend so readily to the whims of the American bureaucrats? He was hardly the man she remembered from her youth. Not at all.

He was stronger then, and bolder, more creative, open,

and willing to listen. Now he appeared closed minded, protective and catering. It was embarrassing to see him that way. She had sat in the meeting the day before with that sinister looking Presidential Aide named Morely who made it dictatorially clear that anything so alarming as Jill's recent discovery was not to be made public until such time as the American President had decided. What was that all about and why did Rouard agree to it? A few years back he would have given the information to the media himself, career or no career. And why did she sometimes feel the way she did about informing the public? Would it be too much for them, as she claimed to have felt, or was Sam right? Did they have a right to know, regardless? Would they be able to handle it? Somehow she didn't have much faith in people anymore, or sympathy for them either, as a matter of fact.

But then again, maybe she wasn't being fair. After all, she had been privileged in many ways. She had been in space, for one thing. One of the first scientists to spend time on the space platform put up shortly after she had finished her doctorate. That was nearly ten years ago but she still remembered it as clearly as if it had been yesterday. All the excitement and intensity, the awesome, delicate beauty.

How distinctly she remembered looking down, staring transfixed for hours at a time. Surely, as seen from above, Mother Earth was a pristine, luminescent, azure jewel. That marvelous planet, arcing through the void around the sun, many factors precisely and delicately balanced to support life on the spinning, cloud shrouded, molten interiored, water covered, slightly pear shaped, wondrous blob of rock called home. The place now seriously endangered because, down on the surface she, Mother Earth, ecosystem sublime, was no longer pristine. Instead, she lay raped, befouled, wounded, sorely abused. Forests slashed, lands stripped away, oceans polluted, and far worst of all, the contaminated atmosphere deteriorating, the balance of ingredients destroyed. The sky a twenty mile thick chemical dumping ground saturated with millions of tons of gaseous, noxious, eye tearing, lung searing, paint etching, cancer causing, by-products of civilization. A

61

lethal, diabolical soup generously flavored and replenished with man made, poisonous condiments, constantly and continuously stirred and circulated by global winds so that ultimately no man, no animal, no creature, insect, fish, fowl, blade of grass or growing tree was safe, no matter how high up the mountain or how deep in the ocean or how remote from civilization was the habitat. Not anymore. Already more than a million species had disappeared, extinct forever, all within the last one hundred years of man's history.

The devastation was everywhere, all in the insane, cowardly name of progress, gross national product, the production of things and accumulation. Man's self granted right of power and control over nature, the self granted right of ownership, to have and use what pleased him. Or not to use, but simply to have because his neighbor had, so he must have too, something at least as good, and hopefully better. The consequent conversion of natural resources into consumer goods all measured in the only criteria that really mattered, the amount of energy it took to produce them, energy in large part derived from the use of fossil fuels. Coal, oil and natural gas, all carbon dioxide producing.

But it wasn't the byproduct of combustion itself that was the problem. Carbon dioxide plus sunlight and photosynthesis, meant trees and plants. Trees and plants provided food for the earth's creatures and produced oxygen. Creatures needed oxygen to metabolize the food they eat. Metabolism, in turn, produced carbon dioxide, round and round. Interdependency, delicate balance, equilibrium, necessary and good, carefully regulated by nature for many millions of years, up until 'man' became 'modern man'. Instead of using judgment and restraint, however, modern man had breed like oversexed rabbits, overrunning the planet, inventing even better and more efficient ways of ripping minerals from the earth in the name of progress, sucking out the oil, stripping the topography of trees and all the while spreading chemical and radioactive poisons in his wake for the sake of the 'economy'.

But what was the economy based on? The manufacture of largely unnecessary, over indulgent goods, over heated swimming pools, over cooled houses, over feed people and over pampered offspring seeking to raise materialism to some god like status, thereby converting the less fortunate and the have nots of the world into equally greedy, self seeking monsters, on and on, raising havoc with the delicate and intricate balance nature strived vainly and hopelessly to maintain. 'Man'. Man destroyed the equilibrium. Man created the greenhouse effect. Man caused the ozone layer depletion. Only man. No one else, nothing else. The 'Economy' at the expense of 'Ecology'. Dammit! Dammit!

She rose angrily from her chair and stood staring out the window at the world, feeling like a bird that had somehow flown in through an open door and was now trapped inside someone else's dwelling. What to do, what to do? If only she could get through to Dr. Rouard. There must be something that could be done. They should be analyzing the situation in more detail, trying to come up with better solutions to reverse the effects before it was entirely too late. But where was he? Off in Washington again, probably. Kissing up to some bureaucratic committee trying to keep his funding intact. Or out fooling around with that appendage of a bimbo he made such a fuss over. Dammit! She needed to think, but, thinking was something that was nearly impossible for her at the moment.

THIRTEEN

"Well, I'm not convinced that it will work. In fact, I don't think it will work at all and I don't see why we would want to fund such a program."

Dr. Rouard stared at the man who was addressing him from across the table. A lean, narrow shouldered man with large, frameless glasses and a receding hairline dressed in an expensive, hand tailored, dark gray, pinstriped suit. And the other one, Burkey. The one with the hair on his face who never said anything, just stared. Goddammit, he thought to himself. How could they treat him this way? But instead of giving him some relief, the man kept on.

63

"As a matter of fact we're not pleased with the performance of UNAAC as an organization at all and we haven't been for some time."

"I'm sorry you feel that way, Mr. Latimer but I don't think a fair assessment has been made of our efforts. What about Doctor Kairns work. Surely that is very significant," Rouard stated and let his eyes include the other man, Morely, who had also joined the meeting.

"Perhaps, but we're very skeptical as to it's validity."

"It's quite valid, I assure you," Rouard said, finding himself in a position where it was to his advantage to defend Jill. Not that she wasn't right. She was. Her work was impeccably done. There could be no mistake. He didn't bring up the fact that someone in the government had taken over the NASA satellites, however, and refused to give Jill any of their data. Why? Because it confirmed her findings, that's why. It had to. But for his own sake, he left that issue alone because he now needed extra funding for his own new, personally conceived project that he hadn't even shared with any of his own people back at UNNAC. Not even Jill. But if the bastards would just listen, he knew he could accomplish something really significant.

In addition to the many square miles of ground reflectors already in place he could further reverse the greenhouse effect with dispersed, high altitude dust clouds. With the right characteristics the dust would reflect a small but significant portion of the ultraviolet and visible light back into space. It would also scatter the incoming, longer wavelengths. In combination, there would be a slow but positive reduction in earth temperature. That, in turn, would be a step towards solving the bigger, more deadly problem. Of course the presence of dust clouds in certain parts of the upper atmosphere would have their own set of lethal side effects for certain segments of the population. But he dismissed that, rationalizing it away, having already convinced himself that, if artificial clouds were only put in place over the oceans, that they would stay in place and not significantly drift over land areas and have an effect on agriculture.

Not knowing what else to say he sat glumly and pondered his predicament. Sometimes the American government grossly confused him. Why didn't all his funding originate from one source. Why didn't congress provide the U N with a sufficient enough endorsement to cover all the projects he wanted to pursue so he wouldn't have to deal with such merciless, impossible to satisfy people as these? NHRF. New Hope Research Foundation, whatever kind of a screen that was. It was still a governmental agency, no matter how you cut it and for whatever reason the administration was trying to hide behind it. And, as for the organizational staff, they were just a bunch of prissy asses, elitist engineers, that's all. Who were they to say that he hadn't achieved something worth while? Who were they to tell him to clamp a lid on Dr. Kairns work? And who were they to say that he shouldn't even have funded it in the first place without consulting them in advance? So what if it had been to his own advantage to suppress her findings at first. Now he needed to use her findings to create some panic, get himself more funding, keep UNAAC alive and functioning and give himself a chance to really prove himself to the world.

Of course his idea would work. Why shouldn't it? He had spent the last two years privately refining his calculations and extending his theoretical model. Now was the perfect time to put it into play. He looked at Morely, right hand man to the President himself, the one who had first ordered him not to make any disclosures about the data who wouldn't even look back at him. What was going on, what was the rest of it? Why wouldn't they listen?

Dammit, Rouard complained to himself. Perhaps he should have taken the time to talk to those Middle Easterners who had made all the overtures. He looked at Latimer. Why had Latimer reacted so harshly when he told him about the Arab's interest. The Arab delegation had presented themselves as genuinely interested and concerned. What difference did it make who one did business with at times like this as long as something was accomplished. It was bullshit. Newhope Research Foundation needed to be renamed to No Hope.

He started to talk again, tried to re-explain everything but they only ignored him further, Latimer thumbing through his papers, Burkey twisting his mustache and acting bored and Morely leaving the room. Damn them.

Moments later Rouard was in a cab on his way back to the airport. Latimer and Burkey had remained at their respective places in the small conference room in the gray weathered, old limestone, governmental office building that Rouard had just left.

"Maybe we should fund his preliminary dust cloud experiments. Let him take it one step farther before we cut him loose," Burkey said to Latimer.

"We can't afford the delay. Since we already know Dr. Kairns' data is valid and will soon make the news anyway, the entire operations time table has to be moved up. So, it's time to discredit Rouard and let him go."

"Do you think it's going to be that easy? The UNACC nations still have a voice in the matter."

"Of course, but with all the doubt and blame we are going to heap on him in the next few days, it shouldn't be difficult."

"What's the status of the unnumbered Bahama account?"

"We already have ten million in it."

"Then I'd better set up another meeting with Massad."

"Good. Tell Massad he can begin to draw on it. And call the owner of the L.A. Mirror. Find out just how much that reporter, Gorhman, has uncovered about the atmospheric problem. Whatever it is, make it clear that the story will go unpublished, at least by his newspaper."

FOURTEEN

Sam put down the thick, loosely bound report of Jill's atmospheric data he had been given by Korsak and picked up the photograph of her that had for some reason been included. Then he leaned back in his swivel chair and put his feet up on his desk, a position more conducive to serious thinking. Thanks Korsak, he said to himself as he looked at the picture that appeared to have been taken in Antarctica or some similarly cold and desolate place. There she was, bless her, head exposed to the wind, smiling into the camera. How the hell did she stand it? If there was one thing he hated more than anything else, it was cold weather. It almost made him shiver to think about it.

But the face, the thought of her, that was something else again. The memory of their evening together swept over him and warmed him until his never silent mind, forever working away, carried him forward into the imagined future and left him surrounded with overtones of regret. He had to publish the information, no matter what. It was too important. But would he loose her in the process? God, he hoped not. How could he make her understand?

He tried to think it through, tried to visualize the two of them together somewhere in the times to come but couldn't get a clear image to form as to how it might all turn out. Then he tried to picture her in New York. What would she be doing now? Was she in a meeting somewhere, was she talking to that asshole Rouard or was she sitting at her desk like he was, thinking of him? Was he important enough to her for that? What did she think of him anyway? Why had she really gone to bed with him? Was it as she had said, she was just horny and he happened to be the lucky guy who happened along and turned her on or was he something special? Could he be something special for her? Maybe there was a chance.

He languored in it for a moment, then shook it off, righted himself in his chair, switched on the computer and then the copy reader. He removed the few pages of summary material that Korsak had attached to the back of the report and fed them in. Ten seconds later the first page of the document appeared on the screen. He reread the compilation and then started editing the material, condensing it down to a half page article of newsprint. When he was satisfied, he hit the print key and ran off a backup copy for himself. Then, half outloud, he said, "Sorry Jill," and commanded the terminal to route a copy to Cliff's office. That done, he rotated around in his desk chair and stared out the window into the hot, smoggy afternoon, wondering what to do with the rest of his day. Nothing, he decided, except to get the hell out of his office and away from work. But he was too late. His computer beeped at him. He turned and read the message on the screen. "Come to my office right away. Cliff."

Sam thought of stalling, of finding some way to get Cliff to come down to his office instead. Keep him on Sam's turf rather than his own. But, what the hell, he decided. The poor bastard was so off balance all the time anyway, so what difference did it make. There would be lots of other opportunities to piss him off. Right now he wanted to see his story make it to the front page. He finished what he was doing, turned back to the window and continued to look out. No point in being too eager. Ten minutes later he got up and headed out of his office and down the hall.

"What do you mean, you want me to go to Argentina? What for?"

"I believe it was your idea to begin with," Cliff said loudly, as his big ears began taking on a dull shade of crimson and appeared to have flattened out against his head.

"Sure, but why now? What about my ozone depletion story?"

"We'll just put it on hold for a while. It'll be here when you get back."

"That might be weeks."

"That's all right."

"No it's not."

"I said it's all right."

"So what's wrong with the story?"

"Nothing. It's a good story."

"So publish it."

"It will wait until you get back."

"Like hell it will."

"It's my decision."

"Bullshit, Cliff. You never made an independent decision in your life. What's really going on?"

Cliff stared at Sam, trying to stay calm. Jesus, he resented this man. Mostly for a lot of reasons that weren't too clear to him but he resented him, nevertheless. Why did he always have to be so damned independent and so cock sure of everything he did? And why is he always bucking my authority. I'm the boss. Christ, he ought to know that by now. Who the hell did he think he was, anyway? Just another reporter, that's all.

Cliff's aggravated mind went on. If he could just get his stubborn father-in-law to listen to him he would have had Sam out of there a long time ago. But the old man wouldn't listen so guess who had to put up with all of Sam's crap? Well, he was getting tired of it. Maybe it was time to talk to his wife again. Perhaps she could put some pressure on the old man. In the meantime however, he supposed he'd better keep it cool.

"Nothing is going on Sam," he said soothingly. "I just want a little time to study it, that's all."

"It doesn't need studying. It needs publishing."

"Well, I'm sorry, but I disagree and that's the way it is."

"Well, I'm sorry too, Cliff, but we'll see," Sam said and started out of Cliff's office.

"Wait a minute. Where are you going?"

"Upstairs to see Hudson."

"You can't do that."

"Why not?"

Cliff hesitated. "Well, because he's out of town," he said.

"Come on Cliff. You can do better than that. I saw his limo in the garage," Sam threw at him and walked away.

FIFTEEN

The UNACC conference room down the hall from Dr. Rouard's office was full. The roster was a Who's Who of eminence. The archbishops of science gathered begrudgingly together to hear Dr. Rouard, their self appointed Pope, the man who had ascended to his position not so much from technical acumen as from political skulduggery. Twenty renowned scientists from all parts of the world sitting around an immense, highly polished, dark walnut table, chattering away like a bunch of squirrels who had just found out that the storehouse cache was less than a quarter full of nuts and an early blizzard was on the way. The organization's funding had been cut. Cut, hell. It had been slashed by at least three quarters because the United States was withdrawing from the organization. How could it? Commitments had been made. Yes and so what? The American President had written another of his infamous executive orders and that was that. And that was not all. Additionally, any and all research data gathered by UNNAC within the last two months had been classified as top secret and anyone who chose to leak it would end up in prison, Americans and foreigners alike. The president had also called Dr. Rouard a knucklehead on social media the evening before, after coming home from a dinner party.

And there he was. Rouard, the man so accused, obviously offended as hell, standing at the head of the table trying to achieve enough order so the the meeting could begin. After his third and loudest, quiet please, he gained enough of an edge to start.

"Thank you," he was finally able to say after banging on the table a few times to gain everyone's attention Skipping his usual welcoming speech because, seriously, he didn't like most of them any better than they liked him, he went directly to the problem at hand. "Well, as most of you already seem to have heard, the organization is in serious trouble financially."

Immediately hands went up with questions while most of the rest didn't bother. They just began yapping amongst themselves all over again, forcing Rouard to finally pound on the table with his fist some more and stare at the violators until silence prevailed. As for providing any real answers as to the what and why of the American decision to withdraw its funding, he didn't have any but it was effective immediately so all he could suggest was some extreme cuts in staffing for the remaining members and a critical review of all the projects they were engaged in.

Instantly a number of huddles again formed as the noise level climbed correspondingly but this time Rouard didn't pound the table with his fist. It still hurt from before so he grabbed the only thing within reach. His open briefcase. Papers spilled out. He ignored them, thumping the case up and down until he got their attention again. Then he made his final announcement. He was leaving the organization.

No, he wasn't resigning. He'd be damned if he would give the damned Americans that much satisfaction after what they had done. He was just leaving. Period. He had better things to do than head up this institute. And, no. He didn't have any recommendations about who should take his place or any of the rest of it, either. They would have to figure that out for themselves, something they vainly tried to do once Rouard had left the room. It wasn't that no one wanted the position. It was because nineteen of the remaining twenty all wanted it. The only one who didn't was Jill who had thus far sat through the entire event without saying a word and at that point got up and left the room.

SIXTEEN

Some things never change, Massad said to himself as he listened to the American. It seriously reminded him of the stories his father used to tell. The ones about his surreptitious dealings to purchase arms from a clandestine splinter group operating under the auspices of the American Central Intelligence Agency back in the nineteen eighties. The only difference now was that, instead of trying to sell his country something, they were giving something away. Not arms, but money. Untraceable money. Money to hire an obnoxious Frenchman and fund some wild scheme for putting dust clouds high up in the atmosphere to block out some of the sunlight.

Allah help him. He didn't like having to be involved with these people because an Arab never forgets. They were the enemy. They would always be the enemy, the despicable meddlers. They had eventually killed his father, two of his uncles and thousands of his countrymen, all because of the staggering ego of the American President and the stupidity and complacency of the American public at the time.

71

So, what were these dogs really up to now? What was it all about and why did the organization he worked for wish to be involved? Whatever it was, he was sure there were bigger things at stake than the few dollars that were changing hands. So be it, however, because while an Arab never forgets, an American forgets that an Arab never forgets, and there is a distinct advantage in that. Unfortunately, for the time being, however, it wasn't his to know or to understand in detail. He was merely complying with the desires of his own leaders.

"Very well, Mr. Burkey," he said to the pale eyed man who had come to see him. "It will be taken care of." He then tucked the notes he had taken during their conversation into the drawer of his desk and summoned his driver to deliver the man back to the Tehran airport.

"Well, well, well," Rouard said out loud as a grand smirk bloomed across his face. All that wonderful money. And most importantly, a chance to show those American government officials what he could really do. They would see all right, damn them. The devious bastards, manipulating everyone the way they had because he had refused to resign good naturedly. Were they stupid? Why would he have wanted to do that?

He had to admit that he had been worried at first, however. What would he have done if the Arabs hadn't been interested in helping him? He would have been a washed up has-been, that's what. But no matter now, it had all turned out for the better. The first big deposit was already in his bank account, with lots more to come. So much for his financial security, his professional eminence would soon follow. He gloated and brushed the palms of his hands together in anticipation of his envisioned, forthcoming success. He could see it already. Then they'd be back trying to get him to head up UNAAC again. After it was properly refunded, that is. But not this time. This time he'd tell them all to politely go to hell.

He smiled again and threw a few more clothes into his luggage. What an opportunity. It was also a good excuse to leave his wife behind for what might be some considerable length of time, but, at the same time he would miss Estelle. All that soft, plump flesh would be nice to have around. For a moment he considered sending for her after he was settled. Then he thought of the dark, warm eyes of the Arab women he had stared at on his last trip and wondered. Certainly customs had changed. They no longer wore veils and were far less subservient than any time in history. He bet they'd make a good tussle in the hay. However, he reflected, the typical Arab male was still pretty much of a hot head. He wouldn't like to see his balls hanging from the top of some Mosque.

With that, his thoughts turned back to Estelle and their last night together. He smiled and snapped the clasps of the heavy bags together, carried them to the front door and sat them down. There was nothing left to do except wait for the taxi that would take him way the hell up to La Guardia where he had to go to catch his long, overseas flight, since both Kennedy and Newark airports were no longer operational because of the high water.

Rouard was quite surprised with the accommodations they had arranged for him. Mon Dieu. It was nice to be treated with some respect for a change. He stood on the small balcony overlooking the bustling turmoil of the street below, hot in the afternoon sun, and thought of himself as Pierre. Doctor Pierre Rouard. That's who he was, Doctor Pierre Rouard, now living in luxurious splendor in a penthouse located in the newer quarter of what was left of old Tehran. He certainly wouldn't miss his New York apartment. No sir. It was absolutely shabby by comparison. Now if he just had someone to share it with on occasion, life would be quite complete. Or so he thought.

His fantasy, however, was short lived for he was given a rigorous, non-negotiable schedule with set milestone dates for the several levels of accomplishment necessary to achieve the mission that he had agreed to. Although his laboratory and the support facilities provided him with every conceivable convenience he had asked for, his schedule left little time or energy to pursue the pleasures of the flesh he had been so accustomed to.

His difficulties were compounded by his inability to

understand the native language which further isolated him from any satisfying interchange with his surroundings. Other than his male interpreter, Massad was the only person he came in contact with that he was able to communicate with. While the interpreter was most accommodating in almost all respects, even accompanying Rouard to the restaurants and the market when asked, he drew a clear, hard line when it came to acting as intermediary between the Doctor and the women he came in contact with, rewarding Rouard's simple questions in those matters with a cold silence.

When he hinted at the matter of female companionship to Massad, Massad suggested that perhaps he should send for his wife. When Rouard tried to explain his poor relationship with his wife, Massad suggested that perhaps he wasn't spending enough time in the laboratory. It was at this point that Massad began stopping in to see him on an almost daily basis with an uncanny precision that coincided almost exactly with the moment Rouard was getting ready to leave for the day. He then proceeded to keep him busy for another hour or two by reviewing his accomplishments and his plan of action for the following day.

As a result, Rouard's frustration turned into a dull, lingering irritability and a crabby churlishness that interfered with his enormous appetite. By the end of the first month a grand total of twenty five pounds had disappeared off his frame and most of his clothes no longer fit, something which no longer mattered without any women around. Instead, all he knew was that he had accomplished a devilish amount of work, far more than he had originally considered possible in so short a time.

Surprisingly, the actual formulation of the dust itself had come relatively easy. They had happened upon an extremely fine grained, low density silica composite that he felt would, once dispensed, probably spread out and stay in high orbit for a period of many years. The staff mathematicians had also exercised his theoretical atmospheric model and computed altitudes and conditions for minimal drift of the dust clouds over the same long time periods. And once it was up there it would have an almost immediate effect of reducing global temperatures by reflecting large amounts of sunlight back out into space before it could be absorbed and produce more warming of the planet.

Yes, he was quite satisfied with those aspects of the problem. What drove him crazy, however, were the more mundane, practical aspects of the mission. How did you manufacture the damned dust in sufficient quantity to do the job. The miserable stuff was so light and fine it drifted into everything. The eyes, the nose, the mouth, across the room and down the hall. Into the ventilating system, everywhere, leaving its smudgy coat on everything in sight. Ultimately, he told Massad, they would have to build a special facility if they were to succeed and produce it in the quantities necessary.

Then there were the containers. What did one make suitable containers out of anyway? How would they ever be able to pack the illusive stuff tightly into the containers once they had them? How would they get the containers to open efficiently once they were in the cold of space, how would they control the rate of dispersion to get the correct cloud densities? And how big were the containers supposed to be, goddammit, and what were they going to loft them into the necessary orbit with? That was a very critical question, the one that bothered him the most. One Massad didn't have the answer to as yet, so every time Massad asked him about his progress, he asked Massad what the launch vehicle configuration was.

After nearly a week of this verbal impasse, Massad came to the laboratory in mid morning and they went in a limo to what appeared to be a governmental building on the outskirts of the city. Inside they proceeded to an office on the top floor that looked back towards the east in the direction of the center of town. Two men in military uniform greeted them. One was referred to simply as, The Leader, who remained behind his desk. The other one's name was Peshadi.

"So Doctor. I am told that you are making good progress," said the Leader.

"Oui, Monsieur."

"In English please. I have trouble too much with that even."

"Yes sir," Rouard found himself saying to the intense looking man whose dark eyes pierced his very brain.

"Tell me about these dust clouds you are making in your scientific playpen," the Leader said.

Rouard suddenly felt off balance and very much on the defensive. It took him some moments to recover. When he did he told the man about the theory of the clouds and their purpose in the simplest of terms he could muster and then reiterated his accomplishments to date.

The Leader frowned and seemed puzzled by it all. "What will happen to these...clouds as you call them once you have dumped them all into the space up there?"

"If they are laid down properly they will spread slightly and cover major portions of the South Atlantic, the Indian Ocean and the South Pacific. Fortunately there are very few people left in those regions."

"So it is. For some of us to survive, a few will have to perish."

Rouard shrugged in acknowledgment.

"How long does it take to become ready?" Peshadi asked.

"It is a very difficult task and as yet I do not have all the information I need to complete the effort."

"Yes, I am told you want to know about the launch vehicle."

"It is important to know that at this time because that will dictate the size and shape of the containers as well as the mechanisms for control and dispersal of the dust particles. From the knowledge I have gained of the missiles in your inventory, it will take a number of launchings to accomplish the mission because of their small payload capability."

The men in the room stared at Rouard for a moment without speaking. "What do you feel would be an ideal solution to the problem, Doctor?" asked Peshadi finally.

Rouard smiled as he thought how preposterous his answer would sound but he told them anyway. "Perhaps we could get the Russians to lend us their space shuttle," he said jokingly. "It would make the entire mission much simpler."

"They would never jeopardize their friendship with the Americans at this time," Peshadi returned quite seriously. "Too much is at stake. However...it is a possibility that we could obtain one of the American machines now that they are back in the business of having their own once again.

Rouard looked at him. The man was obviously quite serious.

"That's impossible," he scoffed. "If the Russians wouldn't give us one, why would they?"

"I believe there is a way."

"What? Steal it? What good would it do? You don't have anything big enough to launch it with anyway."

"My dear Doctor, you speak so harshly. But still, suppose we waited until it was already up there at the space station. We could have your materials pre-parked elsewhere in orbit, rendezvous and load in space."

Rouard considered the ramifications of what he had just heard. Technically speaking, it was not a bad idea. Actually, it was quite good, brilliant, in fact. But politically, Dieu tout puissant, it would be a disaster. Perhaps not for them, provided they didn't get caught in the act. But for him, that was something else again. Everyone would know he had a hand in it. They would know that it was his genius that had made the whole thing possible. Who else? So, instead of becoming a hero as he had planned, he would become an international criminal by association, even if it wasn't personally his idea to pilfer the vehicle. Still, he was curious.

"Exactly how do you hope to accomplish such a deed?" Rouard asked. "Space is more tightly scrutinized these days than the Autobahn."

"To be sure, but we have a sound plan."

"I would be pleased if you would share it with me."

"Of course," the Leader said and turned to his intercom. "Have Dr. Yazid come to my office," he ordered to whoever was at the other end. "It will be just a moment," he said to Rouard.

77

Rouard took the opportunity to stuff a portion of his shirt tail back in and was about to ask for something to drink when the door opened and a cryptic looking, older, brown faced man wearing the typical Arab headdress walked in.

"Ah," said the Leader. "Come and explain to our friend the plan for getting the space shuttle."

"Yes my Leader," said Doctor Yazid in fluent English and walked to a large map attached to the wall across the room from where they were sitting that showed a space view of the earth.

"There is a large old Russian booster still in high orbit following this path," he said and traced the curved line overlay with his finger. "Periodically it swings very close to the primary American space station located here. This will occur in about four and a half weeks and again in nine. We will launch the capsule southward over the pole out of sight to the US and European tracking stations. It will junction with the Russian booster and come around in its shadow hidden from view.

"A clever idea, I must say, but how will someone get to the space station and inside the craft without detection?"

"When in close proximity, our capsule will be guided to drift upward in the shadow of the booster out of sight from ground radar. At the time it will also be on the dark side of the planet and difficult to see from the space station. During closure a high output, infrared laser will be used to...."

Doctor Yasid went on to explain the remainder of the plan to Doctor Rouard. When he finished Rouard said, "As simple as that?"

"Yes, I think so."

"What will we be using as a ground base for lofting the containers of dust prior to that time?"

"Perhaps that island in the Marquises where your government's above ground nuclear testing killed all the Tahitians so many years ago. Not such a nice thing, was it?" the Leader said, prodding Rouard.

"An embarrassment at the time but hardly important now,

I would think," was Rouard's retort.

"Well, you need not worry about it because we have a more favorable location in mind. One not so far away down in the South Indian ocean.

"And what about the crew who will man the craft? I will need some time to train them in the method of dispersal."

"The pilot is our concern. However, for your information he is a very capable, disgruntled American who is highly motivated to help us. As for the payload and other personnel, they will be your concern. Surely Doctor, you would wish to go along?"

Rouard blanched and choked. He was barely able to respond. "I..." he said. "I...doubt if it would be necessary."

"But Doctor," the Leader said. "You have worked so hard to bring your idea into being. Surely you would wish to go along to insure that the mission is a success?"

"I really don't see that it's necessary."

The Leader looked at Peshadi. "Is it possible that we have chosen the wrong individual?"

Rouard squirmed in his chair. Beads of perspiration had already begun to form on his brow.

"I have never been in space before. I'm much to old and physically unconditioned to be considered for such a serious undertaking."

"Perhaps it is time you went then, before you become much older. It will be a grand new experience for you. And in the meantime we will do everything in our power to assist you in improving your bodily condition. Massad has already obtained the services of an excellent physical therapist to guide you in a program of diet and exercise."

"I absolutely object. I refuse to go," Rouard finally stated vehemently, feeling as though he had somehow been sentenced to death. "Mon Dieu. Qui veut noyer son chien l'accuse de rage." He felt sick and betrayed. Nausea swept over him but he was damned if he was going to show any weakness as he fought a compelling urge to run to the men's room and relieve himself.

The other three men in the room simply sat and stared at

him. Feeling liked the trapped animal that he was, he wished he could somehow melt and slip through a crack in the floor.

"Think about your success, your reputation when all has been accomplished. You will be an international hero."

"No, I will be a criminal for being involved in the theft of the shuttle."

"Ah my friend. You are too short sighted. If the mission is a success, who will care about such a minor detail?"

The words calmed Rouard a bit. Yes, he could see that. If the mission was a success and the greenhouse effect was reversed as a result of such daring, well then...then he would truly become the intrepid warrior, the man of courage, a hero. Certainly it was worth thinking about, wasn't it? Still, he remained silent, collecting his thoughts.

"Well, we shall give some thought to finding a substitute for you," the Leader said at last. "In the meantime however, we will proceed with the plans as outlined here. Either way the exercise will not hurt you. You are still much too fat to be living in this part of the world anyway."

Batards, fils des chiennes, Rouard said to himself. Conniving chenapans, devious sons-a-bitches. Changing all the rules of the game they had originally agreed to. Or had they? Maybe they hadn't discussed this part of it at all. God, how could he have been so stupid? He was so used to having others take care of such details and not having to be so personally involved. He was the architect, not some grease ball technician. How could they even consider such a thing?

But they had, hadn't they? And what could he do about it? Nothing, obviously, at the moment. Well, let they play their guerre des nerfs, he would stall and think about it some more. It was just then, however, when he was feeling his worst that he found himself asking a very odd question under the circumstances.

"Where is the landing strip?" he asked.

"What landing strip?" was the reply.

"The place where the shuttle will land when it comes back from the mission."

"It has all been arranged. Everything has been planned

for."

"But I would like some specifics on that part too."

"Doctor, relax. You worry too much."

"I am doing my part. Now that I know how to configure the dust containers, the payload will soon be ready. But before I continue however, I want to know where the craft will put down and what arrangements have been made in that regard."

"Doctor, Doctor. Of course you may know the plan...You will land on a small island near Bora Bora where we have already begun to refurbish the runway built by the Americans way back in World War Two."

"What? Why there, so far way."

"Do the unexpected. Send you up on one side of the planet, bring you down on the other. It's far safer that way, wouldn't you agree?"

"Well, yes. Perhaps. Then what?"

"Then a plane will be waiting to bring you back here. Or, wherever else you might choose to go."

"And the rest of my money?"

"It will be in your private account waiting for you to spend as you choose."

Do leave the shuttle and be returned here to receive the balance of your fee. Then you are free to do whatever you want."

"Are you sure that old airstrip will handle something as heavy as a space shuttle?"

"Why wouldn't it? It's carved out of coral rock. And don't worry. All the work is being done after dark and disguised during the day so the satellites do not see us."

"Well..." said Rouard and waited. There was nothing else he could think of to say.

SEVENTEEN

Rouard's departure from UNACC had come as somewhat of a surprise to Sam. Sure, he thought the man was a blustering, obnoxious opportunist. But he wasn't a complete idiot and seemed securely entrenched in his position through his extensive political connections, thus there was strong reason for Sam to wonder exactly what had happened. Who was behind it and how had they pulled it off. It had to be someone in the U S government since they were the principal backers of the organization. And Korsak had once hinted that there were other government agencies involved. Why was that, Sam wondered, but it was just a passing thought, appearing and disappearing in the multitude of things that were on his mind.

Even though Korsak had been dismissed by Rouard, he would have still been the likely successor to the post because of his long tenure with the Council, had he been reachable at the time the vacancy had occurred. But he was in Russia instead. Schalla had received a brief letter from him promising to return to New York as soon as he could and asking her to give his regards to Sam and Jill. There was no mention of the situation in Russia, however, or how his family had fared in the turmoil or how anyone might go about reaching him. Regardless, he seemed committed to Schalla and somehow Sam knew he would be back, even though it was sometimes difficult to reassure her. But he tried and kept her isolated from his own peculiar set of problems.

He hadn't seen nor spoken to Jill, either, since their one evening together but he had heard through his sources that Jill was finally selected to fill Rouard's position because of Korsak's unknown whereabouts, much to the chagrin of some of the more senior members. The story was confirmed by an article in the New York Times a few days later. Once it was official, Sam picked up the phone and called to congratulate her but couldn't get past her secretary. She kept claiming Jill was in some meeting or other. After the fourth try he gave up. Well, maybe she wouldn't be so unreachable once he found a publisher for his story, he thought. And instead of trying to reach her, that's what he should be doing instead.

But so far, that hadn't been particularly easy. Actually, it was beginning to seem impossible. He was offered a job by three other papers but none of them would touch the story. They all had other assignments they wanted him to work on but each one stated that a story about ozone depletion was of no interest. Somehow it began to sound like conspiracy. But hell, that didn't make any damned sense.

Then he remembered Bill Grisson. Now there was a tough old bird. Sam smiled as he thought of him, saw his knotted face and shock of brown hair. Those steady, calm gray eyes that fathomed everything. How outrageously drunk they had gotten together after they had saved each other's ass in the African bush not too many years ago.

But Bill had done the right thing. He had saved his money and eventually bought a small newspaper in Ohio. The last Sam had heard of him, he now owned two more. Even together, their's was not an overwhelming circulation, but it might be a place to start. Maybe break things loose, get the ball rolling. Sooner or later the big guys would be forced to pick up the story.

Sam smiled again when he heard Bill's voice. "SAM! Goddammit Sam, how are you?"

"Good, Bill. How about yourself?"

"Reaching out, Sam. Not exactly William Randolph Hearst yet but we just bought the paper over in Columbus. Our combined circulation is now over the half million mark. Not too bad for such an old nonconformist."

"Something we need to drink to all right," Sam said.

They spent ten minutes talking about old times and catching up. Then Bill, still the good friend, sensed what was on Sam's mind. "What can I help you with, Sam?" he asked.

"I've got a story you might be interested in," he said and went on to explain the substance of it.

"You're sure it's authentic?"

"Damned right. I have a full copy of the data right here."

"Well, goddammit Sam. Get your butt back here so we can start setting type."

There it was, big and bold. LIFE PROTECTING OZONE LAYER DESTROYED. DANGEROUS CHEMICAL FALLOUT OCCURRING. And it was about to hit the street, all five hundred twenty one thousand two hundred and fifty copies. But he still had to reach Jill and give her some small advance notice, no matter what. But when he called, he got the usual, she was unavailable story from Jill's secretary.

"Leave her a message then," he said. "This is Sam Gorhman. Tell her the story is being published."

"Can I tell her what story, sir?"

"She'll know. And let me give you the phone number here just in case she wants to get in touch," Sam said and gave her the number in Bill's private office.

Jill picked up the pile of yellow message slips stacked on her desk and started to sort through them just as her secretary came to the door and looked in.

"Yes Beverly. What is it?" she asked Rouard's old secretary. Beverly was still with her. Jill found her to be very efficient and enjoyed her callous sense of humor. Beverly, in turn, found Jill to be the most decent person she had ever worked for and gave her the dedicated best.

"There's a reporter on the phone from the Cincinnati herald. Says he needs to talk to you."

"Did he say what about?"

"He wants to know if the story is true."

"What story is he talking about?"

"I assume it's the same story the other gentleman called earlier about."

"What gentleman?"

"Mr. Gorhman, I believe," she said and chuckled.

"What's so funny?"

"He used to tickle me the way he would badger Dr. Rouard. He was one of the few people the doctor couldn't intimidate. Him, and Dr. Kolowski.

Beverly watched Jill's face as she spoke. She could see that Sam's name invoked some interest. "When did he call?" she asked.

"Last thing yesterday when you were in the meeting with those men from New Hope. He left a message and a number. His voice sounded like the same man who called a number of times before. Remember, I told you about it. The phone memo should be in the pile I left on your desk."

Jill began scanning through the message slips again and found the one from Sam. "Oh damn," she said.

"Yes miss. What should I tell him?"

"Who?"

"The reporter on the other line."

"Oh. Yes. I forgot. Let me talk to him."

With that Jill punched the blinking button on her phone. "Hello, may I help you?" she asked.

"This is Charles Schmidt with the Cincinnati Herald. The Columbus Gazette ran a story in their morning edition about a severe ozone depletion effect in the upper atmosphere. I figured if anybody ought to know about it, it would be your organization."

"What exactly would you like to know Mr. Schmidt?"

"Is it true?"

"Do you know the reporters name?"

"I believe it was some guy named Gorhman."

"Then it's true."

"What?"

"The story. I haven't read it but I'm sure it's factual."

"Can I quote you on that?"

"Sorry. Not at this time."

Jill hung up the phone and sat staring at the note with Sam's name on it. The call had come in at three fifteen yesterday. It was now three twenty in the afternoon a day later. Well, at least he had the decency to try and call, but dammit, this wasn't good news at all. Jesus! Now what? She tried to imagine the sound of his voice on the phone when he had talked to Beverly. The vision of his face danced in front of her. She could see his eyes, the dark blue of his eyes, hurt and angry at their last parting. And then a bigger truth hit her.

"Oh my god," she said outloud. The material had been highly classified by the government. Was Sam in trouble for getting it out there? Even more seriously, was she, since it was her data? Or, equally bad, was Korsak? Korsak had been the one to pass it on to Sam. She knew that because he had had the decency to tell her so. But she wasn't angry about it because actually she admired him for his bravery. But was that why Korsak had to gone to Russia? To avoid going to prison? Perhaps, but she seriously doubted it. Korsak would be back, she was sure of it.

She thumbed the phone call memo and tried to sort out her feelings. The last few weeks had been nothing but turmoil and chaos stirred together into some despicable, semi opaque stew of pressure, pretense and politics that had little or nothing to do with science or sanity as nearly as she could see. Or was she misreading all the cue cards? No, the glass was really bent, all the realities were skewed, distorted and discolored. Something was amiss at this level in the world. Manipulation and control was the real name of the game. And ego gratification. No one seemed to care about the real problems.

And what kind of dubious game had Dr. Rouard been playing, anyway, and why had he been so ungraciously forced out of the council? She was convinced that somehow the men, Latimer and Burkey, were connected to it. And what was New Hope anyway, if one got to the bottom of it? That was something she'd really like to know. Was it a front for something else? If so, what? Whatever it was, she didn't like it and she shuddered when she thought of them and their dictates. What good was UNACC, anyway, if it had to try and function under these kind of restrictions? It had no fluidity or freedom to operate. No dedication to purpose was allowed. Play the game or loose the little bit of funding which was barely keeping it alive. That wasn't the original intent at all. How had Doctor Rouard let it slip away?

"God, what a sham," she found herself saying. It was the first time she had fully allowed that thought to surface. But it was the truth. So what was she going to do about it? Go along with it for the time being, probably, since there was no other clear avenue. Thanks to her own research, it was quite obvious that the entire world was in even more serious jeopardy than previously envisioned. The scientific community knew what the immediate problem was but they certainly didn't know what had caused it and until they did they wouldn't know how to go about correcting it. But the real paradox was, why now? Why had the atmosphere changed so dramatically for the worst in just the last six months or so?

World population was at it lowest point ever. Most sources of industrial pollutants had been outlawed in the major countries, gasoline powered automobiles were almost a thing of the past, at least in the United States and destruction of the rain forests had dropped substantially. So what was going on? They had to find out. It would be well worth the sacrifice to endure the politics of her position if they could learn the bigger truth. There was no other alternative except nearly complete extinction.

God, how she wished Korsak was there to help. The man was positively brilliant. And with that, her thoughts again returned to Sam. She had to admit that he was probably correct. For better or for worse, the story needed publishing. However, it still wasn't right to have done it without her permission, no matter what. That was stealing. Or was it? Maybe if she had returned his calls it would have been different.

She got up from her desk and went out and down the hall to make herself some tea. Returning, Beverly scolded her, telling her that it was part of the secretary's job to do those things.

"I'm a big girl," she replied in turn. "I need to get up and walk around once in a while too. And besides, you have better things to do than wait on me."

Beverly gave her a shrewd look. Such a wonderful young lady, she thought. What a pleasure to have her as a boss instead of that vain, demanding, lecherous old man she had replaced. And what a burden she seems to be carrying. Something else was going on too. She asked Jill about the story. What story were they referring to? Then Sam's name came up. Beverly could see the same emotional reaction in Jill as once before.

"Why don't you return his call?" she asked Jill. "Maybe he has an update on what's happening."

"It's possible, I suppose. Maybe I should."

With that, she went into her office and picked up the memo. Yes, she'd like to know what was going on. And, she also admitted, it would be nice to hear his voice again too. She reached for the phone, dialed the number in Columbus and waited. A woman's voice came on.

"I'd like to talk to Mr. Gorhman," Jill said.

"I'm sorry but he's not here."

"Do you know when he'll be back?"

"I believe he left for Washington earlier this afternoon."

"Will he be returning?"

"I can check with Mr. Grisson if you like but it didn't sound like it. Would you like to leave your number in case he calls?"

"No...thank you anyway."

EIGHTEEN

"How the hell did this happen?" Latimer was asking Burkey as he sat looking at a copy of the Columbus Gazette. They were in Latimer's top floor, windowless office where Burkey had just been summoned.

"Obviously Mr. Gorhman didn't give up so easily. Pretty clever actually. If enough other independents pick it up, the wire services will want it too. Then there'll be no stopping it."

"Has the Oval Office been informed?"

"Yes. They're passing the word along."

"How many others have run the story?"

"As best we can tell, maybe five or six. The last report was from Omaha."

Latimer put down the newspaper, reached inside his suit jacket and removed a pack of dark brown cigarillos. Selecting one, he lit it with his lighter, took a long puff, inhaled most of it, leaned back and let it out.

"How's our new Tehran operative working out?" he asked.

"He was in contact with Massad this morning. Rouard

appears to have resigned himself to the fact that he's going up. They have all the containers fabricated and will begin loading them with dust very shortly. The plan is to air lift them to the launch site late this week. The missiles are already there undercover, waiting for the payloads. They plan to space out the launchings to reduce chances of detection."

"How many will it take?"

"Probably three to get the dust up there and the fourth, of course, for Rouard and the pilot."

"Why so many?"

"I don't know. They say that's what they need, so that's what they need. I guess because the stuff is so heavy and there's so much of it. The cylinders are nearly ten feet in diameter and twenty feet long and weigh about forty tons each. Too big and too heavy for their old style boosters."

"Will they fit into the shuttle?"

"In the phase two machine. That's what up there now."

"Is there any problem keeping it there until we're ready?"

"There doesn't appear to be. The normal scheduling calls for the shuttle to remain for another three weeks. Everything's quiet. No one seems suspicious."

"NASA will be pissed when they loose it. There won't be anything in the budget to replace it."

"A small sacrifice for the good of the nation."

"Let's just hope we don't have another congressional investigation. I don't like making key witnesses disappear under these kind of circumstances."

NINETEEN

The dark, rusting old hulk of a freighter rolled gently in the soft swells that washed in from somewhere out in the vast Indian Ocean and made it strain weakly against its mooring lines. The night sky was clear and the quarter moon had just emerged over the horizon. Assisted by a pair of bare light bulbs hung on makeshift lengths of cord, a flat bed semi truck that had been backed out onto the pier was sufficiently visible for loading. Thus far it contained one very large, long round cylinder that had been strapped to the extreme front of the trailer.

The shipboard crane on the foredeck of the boat squeaked and creaked as it swung a second cylinder out over the rail and lowered it downwards towards the waiting vehicle. Unfortunately the crane operator wasn't paying proper attention to the man signaling him from the pier at the moment. Instead, he was straining to see what Doctor Rouard was doing in the dimmer light around in front of the truck. Was that young native girl smiling at the old bastard? And what was he doing reaching for her breast?

"Oh shit," the man then said in Arabic, finally realizing what he, himself, was not doing and pulled hard on the brake lever with both hands, but it was too late. The rapidly descending container slowed considerably but not enough to keep it from banging into the first one already on board the semi trailer. There was a heavy metallic thud that made the truck rock on its springs and caused the suspended cylinder to swing wildly around on its cable and bang the other end before he could engage the lift clutch and bring his load sufficiently high enough up to avoid a third collision.

Before the sound of the first collision had a chance to die out, however, Rouard was around the truck like an enraged bull and began shouting up at the crane operator.

"Goddammit, take it easy you dim witted son-of-a-bitch," he started shouting wildly, waving his arms and continued to shout. "I'll feed you to the sharks if you fuck up my precious cargo you flat headed, sand grabbing nomad," he roared and kept on until the cylinder was high enough to be out of danger.

Once things were under control, the crane operator looked at Rouard in his fury and shrugged. Although he hadn't understood a word that had been directed at him, the message was still very clear. This was one individual he didn't choose to tangle with so he guessed he'd better be more careful.

Rouard then climbed up onto the bed of the truck and inspected the end of the loaded canister then looked up at the one suspended above him. He motioned to the ground man to give him his flashlight which was tossed up. Carefully, he moved the beam of light over the ends of the containers, stood there for a minute in silence and then climbed back off the trailer.

"Bring that asshole down here and get someone up there who knows how to operate that thing," he said as he gestured upwards.

"He only one, boss," the man said.

"Goddammit," Rouard roared. "Well, see that he sets the rest of them down gently our it'll be your brown ass, too."

The ground man shrugged also, for he too understood very little English. Enough, however, to know exactly what Rouard had called them. Another time, big man, he vowed to himself.

Unable to see the look in the man's eyes in the subdued light and shadows, Rouard stalked off to the sidelines and watched them complete the loading, feeling the false security of his new found virility. Massad's physical fitness program had done wonders for him, lightening the load of blubber he had formerly carried around by some forty pounds. It had also converted much of the remainder of it to leaner forms of tissue. Massad wasn't totally satisfied with the results however, but they had run out of time. Besides, what difference did it make as long as the old bastard didn't die before they got him up there.

Once Rouard was out of the way, the crane operator set the container down as gently as if it were a crate of fresh eggs and then quickly retrieved the final canister from the hold of the old ship and handled it equally well. When it was done, Rouard again began to bark his orders.

"All right, get the detonators off loaded and get that old tub out of here. It will be light in two more hours." He then waved at the truck driver. "Get moving, dammit," he said. "Hurry up, will you."

"Goddamn camel humpers," he mumbled under his breath and walked back to the girl who was now standing by the railing of the pier. He put his arm around her waist and pulled her to him. She giggled and looked at the gold chain he wore around his neck, wondering just how far she would have to go to get him to give it to her.

"Do you really trust these bastards," Rouard asked the American twelve hours later. The person who was to pilot the space shuttle, once they had captured it.

"Ha," the man known only as "Swatch" said with a smirk and took another swallow from the beer can he was holding. Lowering the can, he looked closely at Rouard and wondered at such a stupid question.

They were sitting hidden under a camouflage net strung between the trees, waiting until it was dark so they could supervise the loading of the second container into the upper section of the missile that would place it in orbit where it would be waiting for them when they themselves went up. Although the air was stirred by a slight off shore breeze, the day still felt hot and sultry. Although Rouard had changed into shorts and T-shirt, he still complained about the discomfort. The American, who wore only a pair of faded shorts, hardly seemed to notice, however, as he worked his way through an ice chest full of beer.

"Trust them with what?" he asked. "My wife? Thank god I don't have one.

"Sometimes I wish I didn't either," said Rouard.

"What difference would it make? You don't seem to be missing anything, except perhaps that gold chain you were wearing when we got here. Was it worth it?"

"What was what worth?"

"Whatever it was you got from that brown skinned girl."

"Why do you always have to talk like such a peasant?"

"You sure are an arrogant old fart? Does that come from being French or did you pick it up somewhere else?"

"I happen to be proud of my distinctive heritage and I'd thank you not to make disparaging remarks about it."

"Christ, Doc. Come off of it, will you. If we're going to spend anymore time together, you'd better lighten up."

Rouard studied the long, lean, unshaven man who was about ten years his junior. How had he come to be involved in such a clandestine undertaking? Other than for the money, that was? What avenues had his life taken to bring him here? Had he been in some kind of trouble? And where did he learn to operate a space shuttle? Such a feat was a bit more complicated than driving a Volkswagen around the block, now wasn't it. In some respects he envied the man. He had all the markings of an adventurer and a mercenary, something far more exciting than working complicated equations and dealing with political idiots. He was a cool one too, someone he wouldn't want to end up crosswise with, if he could help it. He envied him his looks and his manhood, both. What he had to pay dearly for, this fellow was getting for free. Regardless of all that, the foremost question in his mind was still whether or not the Arabs were to be trusted. Would he ever see the balance of his money? He asked the question again in a more specific manner.

"Seriously?" asked Swatch.

"Yes, seriously," said Rouard.

"All of my money is already in the bank."

"How did you manage that?"

"They took it to Switzerland and deposited it in my account. As soon as I was able to verify the balance I got on the plane to come here."

"That's very clever. I wish I had thought of it."

"It's too late now. Might as well relax and enjoy."

"Yes, but what about the rest of the situation? Do you trust them about that?"

"I know they must want us up there pretty bad or they wouldn't have gone to all this trouble. I also know that the shuttle will be in good functioning order because the people up there already think it will be bringing them back to earth. As for the rest of it, I have no choice but to trust my own skills."

"What about that old island airstrip. Did they really refurbish it?"

"I was there a weeks ago. It looked to be in good shape."

"Is it really long enough to land a shuttle craft on?"

"As long as the drag chute deploys and the brakes don't fail, we will be just fine."

"What does that mean?"

"It's all part of the adventure. Have a beer. You worry too damned much."

"You're positively sure you know how to bring that thing down?"

"A piece of cake, Doctor. A piece of cake."

Rouard shuddered. God, how he hated American slang.

It was dark. They had barely finished their makeshift dinner when they were summoned to the center of the island where the technicians had completed the installation of the final canisters into two of the three remaining missiles. The third would be carrying Rouard, Swatch and one Arab technician into space. The camouflage netting had already been removed from the sight and the majority of launch preparations completed on that evening's missile while it was still lying on its side in the support cradle. They inspected the work as best they could with their battery powered lanterns and agreed that it looked proper. The missile nosecone was then secured in place and the sixty eight foot long, solid fueled bird was hoisted into the vertical position along side the portable gantry.

The antiquated old inertial navigation guidance platform was powered up and leveled while the chief technician took a final theodolite star reading, transferred it into the optical periscope that was attached to the launch gantry and commanded the platform to assume the correct azimuth heading for its planned trajectory. At this point everyone then retreated to the safety of the concealed, underground center and the final checklist was completed. It was eleven-o-five pm. The launch command was given.

One thing about a solid fuel missile, Rouard thought. The son-of-a-bitch didn't waste any time getting off the pad. And after a brief count to about twenty the thing had reduced itself to nothing but a dim, pin point glow far up in the sky. How in the hell would there own bodies be able to withstand the G forces, he wondered as he watched. Even though the unit that would be carrying the human cargo would have a reduced burn rate, it would still be one hell of a ride. The only good thing was that it didn't give much time to get a good fix on the point of origin for the liftoff unless someone was watching, not too far away over the horizon.

One more to go, and then it's our turn, he lamented ruefully. Their last night on the island. And then what? God Almighty. He wished it were over and he was back in New York buying some new clothes. And right now? Christ, he'd give anything for a good bottle of wine and one last chance to snuggle up against his old girlfriend's warm body.

Several thousand miles away on a tiny little island near Bora Bora another crew of Arabians were also working into the night. A clanking monster of a bulldozer, designated the K-12 by its European manufacturer, emerged from its hiding in the undergrowth alongside the island runway and stopped perpendicular to the paved surface. The operator then lowered the immense steel blade, hit the throttle and engaged the forward clutches. The exhaust stack of the beast belched a cloud of dark smoke as the thick blade dug into the superficially renovated surface of the runway and tore up a swath of old asphalt and chunks of concrete as it plowed a furrow across the full width of the landing strip. As soon as he had completed the first pass the operator was guided by flashlight to a new position a hundred feet further down where the process was repeated over again until the entire length of the runway was ravaged by a series of ditches and piles of rubble that traversed its width.

As the bulldozer completed its destructive task Major Hascomb of the South African Air Force stood squarely in front of a large wall map in the headquarters building in old down town Pretoria. A native white Afrikaner, he was briefing his Chief of Staff, the first black man ever to have ascended to such a position in his country.

"They are all here, sir," Hascomb said and pointed to a location over the South Atlantic about two hundred miles due west of Angola. "The third one just came up and is sitting approximately half a kilometer off from the others. All are stationary at an altitude of thirty nine kilometers."

"Again silent?"

"Yes sir."

"Do we have any idea as to the origin of the launch?"

"Somewhere in the vicinity of Rodrigues Island, east of Madagascar and to the south, far enough over the horizon to prevent getting a good extrapolation back to the exact site."

"Damned highly irregular procedure in today's world. What do you make of it?"

"The same, sir. Not a good feeling with it parked so close to our heads."

"Exactly. Have you talked to the Americans yet?"

"I was told to call back in about two more hours."

Approximately seven hours earlier by the clock but two hours of real time later and fourteen thousand four hundred miles away, Colonel Stevens of the US Air Force entered the office of General "Bucky" Simms.

"Sir," he reported. "The third launching from the South Indian Ocean appears to have rendezvoused with the first two."

"Anybody claimed them yet?"

"No sir. Not as yet."

"Is there any air to ground activity from the payloads?"

"No transmissions that we can detect. It's just parked up there along with the others."

"How about the launch site?"

"The infrared surveillance satellite shows what appears to be recent ground activity on a small island in the South Indian Ocean. Extrapolating what limited trajectory data we have backwards indicates that as the likely launch spot."

"What about the Australians. Do they have anything to say?"

"They don't appear to be particularly interested."

"Well, it's very unusual. Let's start low level recon flights over that island."

"Yes sir. Will do. And the South Africans have asked us

for information also, what with it so close to home." Stevens said. "I,ve been stalling them until you could be briefed."

"Good. But I'll have to clear it with the President first," the general replied. "You know how he feels about those people."

"Yes Sir."

"And contact Davis at NASA. If someone doesn't declare ownership of those payloads in the next few damned days, maybe they could free up that precious shuttle of theirs and run by and take a look."

"Will do. Anything else Sir?"

"No, just keep a sharp eye on the recon satellite outputs in the meantime and let me know if anything new develops."

TWENTY

Highway hypnosis, night time enemy on the long, lonesome road. Tires singing their soulless song on the pavement, headlights carving out a pathway through the darkness, the muffler and the sounds of the engine both too loud. The muffler rusted and leaky, the engine old and worn, struggling to stay alive, hammering away, converting reciprocating motion to rotary motion, turning the wheels round and round, on and on, carrying him through town after town that he didn't even remember passing. Monotony, boredom, drowsy haziness dragging him down, the car droning, droning, daring him to fall asleep. Fight it, don't let it get you, no, not tonight. Slap your face, flex your arms, rub the back of your neck, there's still a long ways to go.

Bud glanced at Jean curled up on the seat beside him, her long, dark hair partially covering her face. A dim figure in the weak glow from the dash lights but beautiful nevertheless. He placed his hand gently on her side, felt her warmth, felt her breathe. God, how he'd like to wake her up, have her talk to him, help him stay awake. But he couldn't. Poor kid, Bud thought. She's as tired as I am, maybe more. Will we ever get there?

There was a sign coming up. He shook his head, trying to clear it so it would register. Dalhart, seventeen miles. Somehow they had made it to the Texas pan handle. How, he didn't know. If there had been a sign at the Oklahoma border, he hadn't seen it. Even though the town was shown on the map, he wondered if anything was still there. So many places were just names from the past anymore. Population-zero. The disappearing face of rural America.

His assumption was correct. Nothing but a crossroads and the barely visible remains of what might have been an old roadside cafe off in the darkness. But, two more hours and they should be in Tucumcari. Maybe he could make it that far. Had to get some gas there, too. He wished they weren't so short on money. Might be nice to stop somewhere and eat in a restaurant for a change. Well, at least it should be light soon. It's not so bad once the sun comes up.

What's that up ahead? Looks like snow. No, its sand, a cloud of sand blowing across the highway. He slowed down slightly, was into it sooner than he suspected. Coming awake, he put the brakes on harder, trying to keep the vehicle straight, but couldn't see a damned thing. Slower, slower, almost stopped now. Oh shit, the wheels were off onto the shoulder. The shoulder was soft, he could feel it pulling him to the right, farther out until all four wheels were in the loose, powdery material, quickly dragging the car to a stop, nearly tossing Jean off the seat.

"Goddammit," Bud said.

Jean was instantly awake. "What's wrong, honey," she asked as she sat up. "Oh my god," she said, looking out the window, hardly able to even see the car hood in the dust storm.

"Just the rest of Oklahoma and Nebraska blowing on down into Texas," Bud said and switched off the lights and engine.

"It just came up out of nowhere," he said.

"Are we all right?"

"Nothing serious. We're probably stuck, is all."

"Where are we at?"

He told her.

"I though we were going through Oklahoma City?"

I decided to take the back way across from Wichita to save time and gas. It's a lot shorter."

"What do we do now?"

The wind howled fiercely, driving the grains of sand into the vehicle, abrading away the rust and the little bit of finish that still covered it and blasting micro chips out of the windows.

"If we had some paint, it might be a good time to redo the car. It'll certainly be nice and smooth, once this lets up," Bud said, trying to lighten the moment.

"How about a two tone this time?" Jean said and laughed. Then she asked what time it was.

"Should be light in a couple of hours," Bud said.

"Is it that late. You must be tired. Why didn't you wake me?"

"I thought I could make it to Tucumcari. It's only about a hundred miles."

"Where's that?"

"Where we get back on the Interstate."

"You shouldn't push yourself so hard."

"Just trying to get it over with. Not much we can do now, though, except wait. Might as well get some sleep."

He reached for the blanket that had covered Jeans legs and pulled it up around them. They leaned together, sharing their warmth and were soon oblivious to the sound of the wind pelting the car with the granular debris stripped from the earth.

Sand had seeped its way in through all the tiny cracks and crevices, many of which would have otherwise gone unnoticed. There was a minor drift across the floorboards by the front seat and another on the dashboard. Bud stirred and opened his eyes. There was a fine powder of sand on the blanket, on their clothes, their shoes, in their hair, everywhere. But the wind had stopped and the sun was up.

Jean came awake. Bud got out of the car and looked. It was a lot shinier on one side than the other, all right. There were also minor drifts behind the wheels but that wasn't the big problem. The shoulder of the road was every bit as soft as it felt in the darkness. Getting out was going to be one damned lot of work.

Bud popped open the hood and looked inside. More dust. He removed the cover from the air filter, lifted out the filter and banged it up against the bumper until most of the sand had fallen out. Satisfied, he put it back, shut the hood, got in, started the engine and put it in gear. Forward, reverse, forward, reverse, rocking it gently back and forth. Finally he gained a foot in the forward direction but then no more.

"You try it," he told her and got out.

Jean moved behind the wheel and they repeated the process with Bud behind, trying to push on the forward portion of the thrust, but to no avail. The rear wheels were only grinding themselves deeper. He rapped on the side of the car. She rolled down the window.

"Shut it off, he said, trying to catch his breath.

Jean killed the engine and got out. "What now?" she asked.

"I don't know. Maybe someone will come along."

They waited. A car came by, then another. And a van and another car, but no one stopped. It was as if they were invisible.

"Do we look that bad?" Jean asked angrily.

"No, it's just the times. Everybody is afraid."

"Afraid of what? We aren't going to hurt anybody."

"Unfortunately, they don't know that."

"Of all the times when people should be helping each other, now is certainly one of them. No wonder the world is a mess."

"It's all right. We'll be okay."

Jean didn't respond. She turned and scanned the barren desert wasteland. They had certainly picked a great spot to be stranded, one entirely devoid of vegetation and life. There wasn't a branch or bush in sight for miles. If there had been, she could visualize collecting some of it and putting it under the wheels to gain some traction. But what were they to do? She didn't ask, however. Bud was resourceful. He would think of something.

"See if you can find some flat stones," he told her.

Her questions answered, Jean gathered stones while Bud unloaded enough of their things from the trunk to find the jack and took it out. He made a stack of stones under the center of the rear bumper, placed the jack on top of the stones and lifted the car as high as it would go. Then he made another pile of stones beside the jack to retain the height he had gained, lowered the jack, added more stones under it and lifted again.

"Lean against the side of the car. Keep it from swaying towards the ditch."

With himself helping to hold the car stable with one hand, he operated the jack with the other and lifted the car as high as possible. "Now," he said. "Push it towards the road."

The rear of the car swung on the jack and came down a foot closer to the pavement. They repeated the process once more, then again and once again until one wheel was fully on the roadbed and the other on firmer ground. Jean started the car while Bud pushed on the front. The wheel in the dirt spun a little, then caught. Seconds later they had it backed up onto the road.

Jean got out of the car. Leaving the door open, she went around to the front and watched Bud as he looked under the car to see if anything had been damaged. He rose, said it looked okay. She hugged him. Another car came up the road from behind them, slowing only at the last minute. The driver laid on the horn and swerved around the open door. Jean made an obscene gesture and yelled at the driver. Bud put his arm around her waist.

"Come on silly, help me get the stuff back in the trunk so we can get going."

"God I'm thirsty. Is there any water left?" Bud asked once they were under way again.

"No, it's all gone."

"How about the food?"

"It's gone too."

"Damn."

"Looks like a ranch up ahead. Maybe they can help us."

Bud slowed down and turned in under the archway made of poles over the drive. Bar-M, it said. Fifty feet down the dirt road was a closed gate. A cowboy in a slouched hat stood guard with a rifle. Bud pulled up within a few yards, stopped and got out of the car.

"We're out of food and water," he said. "Wonder if you could help us out?"

The man shook his head.

"How about just some water then? My wife is very thirsty."

"Can't do it."

"What's a canteen of water, anyway?"

"Sorry buddy. We're not here to give handouts to everybody that comes crying down the road."

"For Christ's sake. Nice bunch of people."

"Look pal, if we gave a canteen of water to every poor son-of-a-bitch that stopped, there wouldn't be none for the stock nor for us folks. Now I suggest you get moving before the boss comes along. He'd have me put a hole in you."

Bud stood and glared at the man. "Well, tell him to kiss my ass," he said and stood there a few steps away.

Watching from the car, Jean put her head out the window. "Come on, Bud. Let the big, intrepid warrior have his way."

The cowboy turned to look at her as he pulled a bullet into the chamber of the weapon.

"Watch your face, bitch. Or I'll blow your lights out," he said and began swinging the rifle around. But he was much too slow.

Bud had the barrel in his hand long before the cowboy could react and lifted it swiftly upward as his knee caught the man in the groin. The grip on the weapon relaxed and Bud jerked it away. The cowboy swore and stared at him. Bud swung the rifle hard into the man's ribs. There was a fracturing crack of bone as the man groaned and went down. This time he stayed there. Bud pointed the gun at him. "I didn't hear you apologize to my wife," he said.

The man stared at him through the pain. Bud prodded him with the barrel. "I'm sorry," he heard the man say after a moment.

"Thank you," Bud said as he raised the rifle and emptied the full fifteen round clip into the Bar-M sign over the gate, blasting it to bits. Then he laid the empty weapon on the cowboy's lap and took the full canteen of water he had with him.

The episode behind them, they drove on, hours and endless hours farther, watching the miles of parched landscape go by, trying to ignore their hollow stomachs.

"How much longer?" Jean finally asked.

"Kayenta's not too far down the road and then we're practically there," Bud said and looked in the door mounted rear view mirror. "But that's not what worries me."

"What's wrong?" she asked and turned, trying to see over the pile of clothing and boxes that filled the back seat.

"The engine. See all the blue smoke coming out the exhaust?"

"Not good, huh?"

"Not good at all." He looked at the dashboard. "Don't like that clatter it's making, either. Sure wish they had put an oil pressure gauge on this thing."

They sat in silence once again, mentally nursing the car along with their prayers at reduced speed. Half an hour later they rolled into what remained of the town. A hollow hulk of an old motel, an abandoned gas station, the windowless, weathered structure of a former restaurant and a few ramshackled, but lived in, houses. Bud eased the car to the side of the road and shut off the motor.

He added two quarts of desperately needed oil to the engine as Jean stretched her legs. Then he slammed down the hood and they got back in. "Ready?" he asked as she pulled her door shut.

She nodded. He hit the starter and put the car into gear. "Keep praying," he said as he eased it gently upward in speed.

Ten miles down the road the oil pressure warning light suddenly showed red on the dash, followed by an immediate, metal to metal, hard knocking sound that ended in silence.

"Oh shit," Bud said, and let the dead machine coast to a stop, pulling it off onto the shoulder as it went. "Well, that's that," he said as they got out of the car and Bud leaned up against it.

"Aren't you going to look?" Jean asked.

"Not much point. We lost a rod bearing or two," he said, staring up the road at the unending, empty highway which disappeared into the terrain some twenty miles away. Behind them it was nearly the same.

"I hope you like to walk," he said.

"Someone will come along."

"But will they stop?"

"They'd better."

Half an hour later they saw an approaching speck coming towards them in the distance. "Let me see what feminine allure can do," Jean said and moved out farther onto the roadway.

By the time the speck had turned into an old pickup truck, she was waving. It pulled alongside and stopped. Thank god it was an Indian, Jean said to herself. She went to the windowless vehicle and leaned in, talking to the brown, weathered features. It took a while. Finally, the man nodded his approval. Bud grabbed two heavy suitcases from the trunk of the car and threw them in the back as Jean removed some of her more prized possessions from the back seat. Bud locked the doors and they climbed into the cab of the pickup, being careful not to tear their clothes on the tattered remains of the seat with it's exposed springs.

"Well, at last we get to meet your handsome cowboy," Dawn White Eagle said as she ushered Bud and Jean into her humble but orderly, three room house.

"Trent should be here any moment. He's down at the

Indian Affairs Bureau trying to help a friend who got in trouble."

Dawn, heavy, but still pretty, chatted and made them hot tea and sandwiches. Jean took a quick bath, finishing just as her brother-in-law arrived, surprised to find them there because there was no vehicle parked outside.

"How did you get here?" he asked. "Where's your car?"

"Down the road a bit," Bud explained.

"We'd better not let it sit long, or there won't be much left."

"There isn't much left the way it is but it's probably worth salvaging. Maybe we can get it running again."

"Why do you want to go to California, anyway," Trent asked once they had retrieved Bud and Jean's old car. "Why not stay here with us until things settle down."

"Bud has an interview at the new hydroponics research station near Santa Barbara next week. If we can get the car fixed," Jean said.

"If it was a Ford or Chevy, it would be easy," Trent said. "Unfortunately ...."

"Yeah. I know," Bud agreed.

Still they decided to drive down to Flagstaff the next day, after Bud and Jean had some sleep to check out a couple of big salvage yards that were there and look for a replacement engine. In the end, however, they were not to be so lucky and two days later they again piled into Trent's truck and drove back down to Flagstaff. There they left Bud standing at the I-40 on ramp with one small piece of luggage and his thumb pointing west, determined as ever to make a new life for himself and Jean.

TWENTY ONE

Although he had been in Washington dozens of times since he had become a reporter, it was the first time Sam had been down Pennsylvania Avenue in a number of years and he was surprised to find that the old White House was now completely gone and a new building in its place. Too bad. It should have been preserved just the way it was, the way a disgruntled band of American citizens had left it after blowing out half the walls and setting it on fire. It should have been an important lesson, but was it? In the long run, had it changed anything? It didn't seem so. Presidents and politicians were just as self serving as ever. Perhaps even more so. Power, greed and control, the same old bywords.

And all the psychotic underlings, they were still around too. Convince them of a cause, either real or imagined, and they would rape, rob, run drugs, steal or assassinate their own mother if it suited their purpose, circumventing both God and the Constitution in the process. Yes, little had changed, even in the face of such overt acts as this. The former home of presidents might now be the site of a new library but something still smelled in Washington. What was it this time? Sam wondered. It was the question he had come to ask of older, owlish looking Jed Smith whom he met at the Capital Bar a short time later.

"Don't tell me you expected things to be different?" Jed asked him back.

"I guess it was foolish of me, wasn't it?"

"The old gang of thieves may have been assassinated by the vigilantes but all the dirty handed little followers were still around waiting to pick up the pieces. A new top dog rises to the surface and off we go again. As to what exactly is stirring this time, I don't know. But I do know that this president is just as surreptitious as the previous one. Maybe more so. Obviously, you have had a problem. What is it?"

Sam told him how there had appeared to be a high level conspiracy to keep the atmospheric story from going any further. Out of the papers and off the news channels..

"That was yours, huh? Good for you," Jed said and smiled at him. "Pretty damned scary though."

"It was supposed to be."

"What makes you think someone deliberately tried to cover it up? And why?"

"When old man Hudson, himself, the man who owns all

106

the stock in the L.A. Mirror wouldn't publish it, I had to suspect something. Nor would any of the other majors. I did some heavy digging. Looked into the various sources of UNACC funding also. Among others, an organization called New Hope came up, but it's not listed anywhere as an official agency, governmental, public or private. After while it begins to look like the Tri-Lateral Commission is still in existence, along with a still wayward CIA, hard as it is to believe."

"Not so hard at all," Jed said.

If anyone should know, it would be Jed. Although he had left his own FBI job early in his career he still maintained his old contacts. Free lance, but still a man loyal to his country and the constitution. As for the rest of it... That was his real dream, Sam suspected. An underground, grass roots return to fundamentals, that was what Jed secretly worked for. And although they never talked about it, Sam suspected that Jed had been the unrevealed source of a couple of blockbuster stories that had shown up in his mailbox a few years back.

"As for the why of a cover up, I have no idea," Sam told him. "That's where I thought you might help."

They discussed the matter a bit longer. "Where you gonna be?" Jed asked.

"I'm staying over at the old Charthouse."

"Good enough. I'll give you a call," Jed stated in departure. Except there was no call. There was no Jed either, when Sam went looking for him. His phone was disconnected, there was no new listing and his old flat had a new tenant in it; a younger man who claimed he had been living there for over a year. Nothing. It was as if he had never existed. Dead ended, Sam went home to California and shared his thoughts with an old friend.

Dr. Sheckman was a good man, a general practitioner in a world of specialists, something he preferred to be. Affordable and human, with an outlook that encompassed both the body and the mind since, as he believed, both are inseparably involved in all aspects of the maladies that befall mankind. Deal with people as an integrated whole. Don't split them up

107

into parts and try to make them well. It doesn't solve anything. That was his philosophy, anyway, and it obviously worked because he had very few long term patients. Get them in, get them well, get them out, was his motto. Nobody hooked on drugs, no long term dependency on the doctor encouraged or allowed, either.

"So what do you think it's all about?" Sheckman asked, after Sam told him about Jed's disappearance.

"At first I thought it might be Rouard pulling strings to keep it quiet until he had a chance to do his theoretical homework, but he's been long gone and no one knows where he is either. Then I thought it might be the government waiting until they could figure out who to blame the crisis on. But obviously, when a man like Jed just disappears, it has to be a bit more sinister."

"Are you in any danger?"

"It's doubtful. The story is out. And as long as I don't get too close to who's behind the rest of it, I should be okay."

"Tell me you're going to leave it alone. You will, won't you?"

"I wouldn't think of it."

"Goddammit, Sam."

"Don't worry, I'll be discreet. And cautious, now that I know what game we're playing. In the meantime the public is finally becoming alarmed so I'll keep that end of it stirred up with articles on the projected, long term effects of Dr. Kairns' discoveries. Maybe something will shake itself loose."

"Don't you think they're stirred up enough?"

"No. Most people are still far too complacent from my point of view."

"They are probably in denial. The human mind only seems to be able to handle about so much difficulty."

"Under the circumstances, that's no excuse. The future of the race is at stake."

"Yes. But if they can't handle it, what do we do?"

"If it comes to that, be prepared to take care of ourselves."

"Like our little survival scheme? Start stocking supplies?"

"Maybe so. But we'd need more than that."

"Like what?"

"Other people with some necessary specialties in key fields. Equipment, a safe place to hole up in, all of it. I'll give it some more thought," Sam stated.

"And how about you? Have you found anyone you'd want to take along?"

"Damned right. Only I don't know how willing she'd be."

"Why not? Haven't you discussed it with her?"

"I haven't seen her in a month. I'm not sure we parted friends."

"What's so special about her, then?"

"For a start, she's absolutely beautiful. She's also an atmospheric physicist. That might come in damned handy."

"Where is she now?"

"New York."

"So why are you here, wasting your time talking to me?"

"Yeah, I see what you mean," Sam said and was quiet. Even if world conditions remained unchanged, there was nothing that he wanted better than to have Jill in his life. And now that the subject had come up, maybe the survival idea deserved to be taken more seriously.

As if in answer to that, Sheckman asked, "Who else would we need, in your opinion?"

"We have the doctor, you, and the psychologist, your wife. I know something about weapons and navigation, I hope. I've also lived in the desert, the jungle and who all knows where but someone with a background in agriculture and animal husbandry would be of value. Additionally, maybe a chemist, a carpenter, a mechanic and, what else?"

"An electronics expert and somebody multilingual."

They were silent for a while, each thinking along the same lines. "Maybe a large sailing vessel would be the thing," Sam stated, having come to a conclusion. "One big enough to live on until we found a safe place. If it comes to that."

"If it comes to that," Sheckman repeated, hoping to God it didn't.

TWENTY TWO

Much to Jill's chagrin, the UNACC council meeting wasn't going well. Not well at all. They were too diverse a lot, too scattered, too unscientific and definitely too political. Instead of taking an earnest interest in the serious technical problems facing the planet as a whole they selfishly only attempted to further their own personal agendas instead. Some of them were also so oblivious they hadn't even read any of the technical reports, of which by now there were several. They were only there to take advantage of a free trip to New York, its night life and their generous expense accounts.

Good god, she began to think shortly after they had begun, maybe it was time to submit her own resignation. Or, just walk away like Rouard had done. Then she could go back to Australia and devote her energies to trying to understand the cause of the deadly anomalies in the atmosphere before they got much worse. Since it was primarily a southern hemisphere phenomenon, perhaps she could at least get the attention of her own government.

And if that failed, what then? Find herself a good looking man, move to Canada where it might be reasonably safe when things got really bad, drink a lot of wine, have a lot of sex, learn to sew and knit, read all the books she'd never had time for and.... And to hell with it. Damn right. To hell with it, she decided then and there, got up and walked out of her own meeting, the one she had called together. She just got up and left the experts. The ones who keep arguing amongst themselves about who's country most deserved to add extra members to the grossly oversized membership and how much of a raise in salary they should be getting in the coming year.

Failing to even close the door behind her, she headed down the hall to her office, quickening her pace, determined to get rid of her briefcase and disappear for the rest of the day. To hell with all of it, she repeated to herself again. Let me out of here.

Arriving at her office, she walked past Beverly without speaking, flung open the door to her inner sanctuary and

110

barged in, nearly falling over the person who was already rising from the upholstered chair in front of her desk.

"Korsak!" she said when she had looked at him. "Korsak, is it really you?"

"Ja," he said and hugged her strongly. "None other."

They sat and looked at each other for a long moment before the many questions started. Hers came first. How was the trip?

He had just gotten in that morning, he said, completely unable to find any trace of his family. Their home town had been almost totally destroyed in the fighting and the guerrillas were moving westward towards Moscow. They were heavily armed and well trained in the use of technological weaponry, some of which was clearly of American manufacture. How they had gotten their hands on it was a mystery. Anyway, since his family was presumed dead, he had, with great difficulty, managed to get back out of Russia and had returned to New York where he might still be of some service.

Jill felt so sad for him when he talked of his family, as the emotion rose up from deep inside, wishing there was some comfort she could give him, she who also had none of her own. She expressed her sorrow as best as possible, however, and told him she was glad he was back. There was much to be done.

"And did you know the story was published?" she asked.

"Yes, it even made the headlines in Moscow. I hope you will forgive me. Are you unhappy about it?" he asked with embarrassment.

"Because you gave the report to Sam?"

"Yes."

"No, not anymore. I can see that it was the right thing to do and I'm glad you had the courage to do it."

"How did you find out it was me?"

"I wasn't sure. It could have been any of the members but you were the only one who tried to get me to see the importance of releasing it, even against Dr. Rouard's objections. I wish I had listened."

"So, we are still friends then?"

"Always."

"And what about Sam? Have you seen him recently?"

"Not since before you left."

"Forgive the question but is that what you want?"

"I...Well, I missed all his calls and now he's in Washington or somewhere..."

"Would you object if I tried to reach him. Perhaps we could have a reunion or something. You could meet Schalla."

"Do you think he would come?"

"Of course."

"But how will you reach him?"

"Talk to his computer in California. He has a house on the west side of Los Angeles near Santa Monica."

With that resolved, the discussion turned to technical matters and it was early evening before Korsak finally excused himself because of his date with Schalla.

Sam was relieved. Although they had found their way to the restaurant separately, Jill seemed receptive to the fact that he was there. Schalla, of course, was radiant in Korsak's presence and Korsak was in good spirits in spite of the tragic disappearance of his family. The conversation chased its way back and forth across the table, maintaining a light mood through the main course and into desert. Ultimately, however, in spite of all attempts to keep it otherwise, it inevitably had to come back around to the problem at hand. In that regard there was one question that needed answering before any solutions to the overwhelming dilemma could be arrived at.

"So, what has changed?" Sam asked, once the subject came up.

"In what regard?" Jill asked.

"Something must have triggered such sudden, further ozone depletion, which is at the heart of it all. What planetary changes have occurred during the last couple of years?"

"Nothing, particularly. Except slightly for the better. Excluding naturally caused forest fires and some slash and burn agriculture in certain areas, all other rates of pollution have diminished, if for no other reason than world population has diminished. Additionally, the ground reflectors have been put in place in the Chile, Argentina and Brazil, southern Africa, some south Pacific islands, New Zealand, a huge amount in Australia and a few in the southwest of this country," Jill stated.

"Why? What are they for?" Schalla asked, being the non technical member of the group.

"To reflect solar radiation back into space and reduce earth temperature," Jill explained.

"These reflectors," Sam said. "Placing them on the ground was a compromise measure wasn't it? Ideally they should have been in high orbit, as I remember?"

"That's true. Then they wouldn't have had to be reflective either because they would have blocked all the sunlight directly. And the shadows they cast on the ground would be even larger than their actual size. But there was no other choice, I believe. Is that correct, Korsak?"

"Yes. It would have been much more efficient and required much less total area if there had been a way to get them up there. In high orbit it would take less than twenty percent of what we now have on the ground, but, since we are talking of millions of tons of material in all, the technology to lift and place that much mass in space just doesn't exist. Not yet, anyway."

"Even if they were made of a very thin film?"

"Even then. And it would have to metallic because plastic would degrade quickly above the denser atmosphere. Even so, if something could have been lofted and spread out it still wouldn't have worked."

"Why not?"

"By the very nature of it's lightness it would bend under solar pressure and drift. Both away from the original location and downward. It would slowly drift over populated areas, putting them in total darkness for years, Eventually it would come to ground."

"I see your point," Sam said. "If a few hundred square miles of it fell on a city, it could effectively smother it."

113

"It could also destroy power lines, clog waterways and generally create havoc. Is that a good term, havoc?" Korsak asked.

"It sounds perfect to me," Schalla said. "Even though I understand very little of what's been said so far."

"I'm sorry, my dear," Korsak said. "We will change the subject."

"No, please continue. I'd like to know more about it."

"How large are the ground reflectors?" Sam asked.

"As I remember the numbers, they cover about a hundred thousand square miles in all.

They sat silently for a while, thinking their separate thoughts about the subject until Sam spoke again. "Okay," he said. "So out of necessity we have thousands of square miles of reflectors on the earth's surface reflecting solar radiation back out into space?"

"Yes."

"And these reflectors have a metallic coating?"

"Yes, again."

"Well," Sam stated. "If I remember some basic physics, metallic reflection causes polarization at certain wavelengths, does it not.?"

Jill and Korsak looked at each other simultaneously, then both looked at Sam, a surprised expression on their faces.

"What?" Sam said and shrugged.

"Nothing," Jill said. "Please go on. What are driving at?"

"I'm not sure. It's just that I vaguely remember something about polarized light having an effect on other things. Is that a possibility somehow on...well, not the normal constituents of the atmosphere but....., he said and shrugged again as Jill and Korsak looked at each other in shocked realization.

"My god," Jill said.

"Ja, goddamn," Korsak stated as they all fell into silence as the bigger realization of what had just been suggested began to sink in.

At that point the discussion between Jill and Korsak turned technical and it was agreed that Korsak would be the one to look at the chemical aspects of the situation. In particular he would try to find out specifically what it was that was gobbling up all the singular oxygen atoms and causing the upper atmosphere depletion. Jill, in turn, would begin preparing a presentation she could give to the government officials of those nations which had reflectors on their land and try to convince them of the urgency for their removal. That, of course brought up the question of who would ever be able to pay for such a momentous task. Would it be the United States? Probably not. Especially after having footed most of the expense of putting them up.

"But they don't have to be dismantled," Sam assured the rest of the group. "The quickest, simplest and least expensive thing would be to use crop dusters. Instead of insecticide, fly over the panels and put down a layer of fast drying paint. Or, tanker planes. The kind they drop chemicals on forest fires with. They could be dismantled and the material recycled later."

"Good," Jill and Korsak agreed. That would be an expeditious solution to that part of the problem. But then, after a few moments of reflective silence about the entire situation in general, another really shocking possibility came to light.

Again Jill said, *my god* as Korsak repeated his, *Ja, goddamn* and Sam added, *those sons-a-bitches* while Schalla simply looked puzzled and asked, what?

Sam was the first to answer. He only said one word. "Conspiracy!"

The group sat in silence for a few moments longer this time, pondering the sinister implications of that one lone word. Over ninety five percent of the reflectors were in the southern hemisphere. So was the greatest amount of ozone depletion by far and that, quite obviously, could not just be a simple, unhappy coincidence. But even so, why would anyone want to specifically put the southern hemisphere in jeopardy? That did not make any sense. And without pre knowledge of the adverse affects of the reflectors and a conscious intent to use that to some sinister end, there would be no conspiracy. Just a glorified rush to judgment based on incomplete research conducted and avidly promoted by one Dr. Pierre Rouard. Or,

God help them all, was there more to it than just that?

Jill was skeptical about Rouard having known of the reflectors side effects in advance. Otherwise, why would he have gotten her the funding to do the study to begin with? Even though he was the one who promoted and pushed the idea to start with, she felt it had more to do with the over inflated egotist he had become than any real desire to help save the world.

Korsak nodded in agreement and added that as he remembered it, Rouard hadn't had a preference for reflector locations at the time. What did he care? He was only too happy to have them built and let some federal agency take over that responsibility. Which one, he no longer remembered.

Jill then pointed out that Rouard had also been criticized by those two government officials, Latimer and Burkey for even funding Jill's research to begin with, without any up front notice to them about the program. That, coupled with the military taking control of the NASA satellites and clamping a high level security classification on all atmospheric data that had thus far been gathered, had to mean something. Something not good.

Damn, Sam said to the group. How he wished he still had some contacts at Wright-Patterson Air Force base. Someone in ARPA, the Advanced Research Projects Agency, the most likely funding source for such a covert program. Maybe more comprehensive reflector research had already been done. Maybe that research had already discovered the reflector side effects Rouard had failed to witness because he was in such a hurry to promote his own self serving agenda. What then? Rouard would have been duped by his own shortsightedness. But even so, why would he have been given funding and allowed to proceed? That now became the really pertinent question. Why would anyone? No, not anyone. Why would someone in the United States government permit, allow or set out to deliberately put millions and millions of people in the southern hemisphere in severe danger and literally pass a death sentence on them? By the time this question came up, however, it was past closing for the restaurant and the

116

employees were politely trying to point that out as they worked cleaning up around them.

Outside the doorman asked how many taxis they would need.

"Two," Korsak stated before anyone else could reply. Then he looked at Sam. "You are going to see the lady home, aren't you?" he asked.

Sam turned to Jill. She nodded in the affirmative. Then, as they waited, Jill talked with Schalla a bit, said she was glad to have met her and then told Korsak she would see him in the morning.

"First thing in the morning," he replied.

"But not too early," Schalla said to Korsak, putting her arm through his. "The world can wait a few hours longer."

"Yes, how foolish of me," Jill replied apologetically and looked at the couple, realizing it would be their first night together since Korsak got back from Russia.

"One for the road?" Jill asked Sam at the door of her apartment. "Isn't that what Americans say?"

"That would be nice," he said.

They went inside. He sat on the couch, she turned on some music and went into the kitchen. "Brandy?" she asked.

"Yes, please."

He waited. She brought the bottle and glasses. He poured, handed her one and lifted the other in salute. "It's nice to see you again," he ventured.

"Thank you. I'm glad you came."

They looked at each other as Sam's heart churned. "I'm glad your story is becoming a success," she said politely.

Was she serious, Sam wondered. She sounded serious. He hoped so. "Are you serious?" he asked.

"Yes, I am. I'm happy for you."

"But what about you? This might still have harmful ramifications for you."

"No, it's too late for that."

"You're sure?"

"Quite. They had to know they couldn't keep it quiet much longer."

"Who knew they couldn't keep it quiet?" Sam asked, surprised at her reference to someone who sounded specific.

Jill explained her encounters with Latimer and Burkey and the foreboding implications that now had for her. In exchange, Sam told her about his Washington trip and the disappearance of his friend, Jed.

"Sounds so sinister," Jill said. "Do those things really happen in America?"

"Damned right."

"But what was so important about this? To want to keep it quiet, I mean. Unless....."

"Yes. The longer it was kept quiet, the more damage the unfiltered sunlight would do, the more human casualties in the end."

"Good god."

"I know. It doesn't even seem possible that anyone could be that evil, does it? But what if it's true. Who's going to believe that story, even if we can get to the bottom of it?"

"But you're the one who will be digging into that side of it. Do you really want to take the risk?"

Sam merely looked at her without answering, staring into her eyes. "Come here," he said at last.

"What?"

"Come sit closer," he repeated and she moved in his direction.

They met in the middle of the couch. He took her drink, sat it on the coffee table next to his and kissed her once, then again.

"I thought you'd never ask," she whispered.

"I wasn't sure you were still interested."

"I'm not. But do it some more, anyway."

He kissed her some more. He kissed her until at last she said, "Dammit."

"What's wrong?"

"I'm horny again."

118

Later, lying side by side in her bed, Sam asked, "Have you always been so frank?"

"What do you mean?"

"Remember walking down the street that first time and you said you were horny?"

"Of course."

"And tonight you said the same thing?"

"Well, is that so bad?"

"Not at all," he said as he ran his fingers slowly and delicately up over her tummy, across her breasts and to her face. "No, quite the contrary," he confided. "It's one of the things I love about you."

"What?"

"You don't mix things up."

"Like what?"

"You don't play games. You know what you want and when you want it and you're honest about it. You don't bargain with sex."

"You're right. I don't put a price on myself."

"And I respect you for it. It's wonderful."

"I'm glad. So with that in mind, can we do it again?"

TWENTY THREE

"That's rather astounding, isn't it? Korsak stated the following morning as he punched the computer keyboard and then pointed to the center of the monitor screen.

"Are you surprised?" Jill asked.

"Only a little, I guess. I wonder why none of us ever thought of it. Too close to the problem, perhaps."

"Or too busy trying to resolve political issues."

"Quite possibly. What do we do now?"

"Two things. Throw a party for Sam for opening our eyes and go and brief the White House."

"Why would we want to brief the White House?"

"It was Sam's idea. See how they react to it. See if there is any indication at all as to whether or not they may be involved."

There were six people in the small, darkened conference room where Jill was standing at the head of the table to begin her briefing. Those seated were General Barnes of the Airforce, Dr. Stein, advisory staff scientist to the President, Korsak, Mr. Latimer and lastly, Sam Gorhman. He wasn't there by official request, however. Rather, it was Jill's determined insistence that he be allowed to attend. Such permission was only granted after a clear understanding that the meeting was classified and not to be used for news copy. Then, when Jill was about to turn down the lights and begin her presentation, the door opened and the President himself came in and sat down at the far end of the table. He looked at Jill and frowned, as though her presence dissatisfied him while Jill, in turn, did her best to suppress the shock she felt. She knew from pictures that he was not a pretty man but in person he was a stern looking, distorted version of Richard Nixon but with orange hair like Donald Trump who nodded at her as if that was the signal to begin.

Pointer in hand, she moved back and forth in front of the projection screen, providing narration for the film strip that was being shown. In spite of feeling uncomfortable in the man's presence, her voice was clear and precise with its trace of Australian accent lending a certain music to it. At least for Sam while the rest of the audience seemed to be concentrating on the material she was presenting.

"This is the Australian network, the largest of all, covering thirty thousand square miles," she stated, showing sheets of polished aluminum panels stretched along the ground, running for miles off into the distance and then worked her way down through the list, down to those located in the American southwest, the smallest of the group by far as Sam studied faces and looked for subconscious reactions as Jill continued.

"The purpose, as you already know, was to reflect sunlight back into space to reduce global warming. It was a compromise solution at best but it did have a verifiable effect. Unfortunately, while it was beginning to solve one problem, it created at least one other that is now very immediate and extremely serious."

At this point General Barnes rudely interrupted by asking Dr. Stein just how the Australians happened to have found out about this before their own scientists had? At first Stein seemed at a lose for an answer and before he could reply, the man named Latimer answered.

"They didn't," he assured the general, pointing out that it was American dollars that funded the study through UNACC to begin with. That settled, Jill was ready to move on when Stein, possibly in an effort to save face, began questioning the validity of the claims Jill was making.. Did she have verifiable proof? Where was the evidence?

"Let me show you," Jill stated as she skipped ahead in the presentation and stopped at a page that showed a long scramble of hand written chemical equations. Then she showed them photographs of the actual apparatus that had just been used to conduct laboratory experiments with, along with more complex equations and lists of the actual data derived from that set up.

"Wasn't there any indication of potential problems before the reflectors were put down?" Dr. Stein interrupted, trying to keep the meeting within channels.

"Not according to the original atmospheric model," Jill assured him.

"The model some members of the council took issue with at the time, is that correct?" Stein said, trying to sound more authoritative than he suspected his appearance portrayed.

"But there was no proof at the time that it was incorrect, either, or as incomplete as it turned out to be, and no one foresaw the bigger problem. Not even the staff at NASA or the University of Colorado consultants," Jill stated, preferring neither to defend or to blame Dr. Rouard for the problem, the original promoter of the idea.

"Dr. Kolowski," the President said, passing over Jill in the process, as if choosing to grant the female member of the group as little recognition as possible. "Can you tell us in more layman like terms what the connection between the reflectors and the... problem, really is?"

"I can try," Korsak said, pausing long enough to make everyone politely aware that Jill should be the one to answer, since she was the present head of UNACC. Jill smiled at him and nodded, the point made.

"The cause is due to the effects of polarized ultraviolet light and surface heating of the reflectors on air pollutants in the atmosphere at ground level."

"Are you sure?" the President asked. "We've had tough laws against air pollution for years," he said skeptically, glancing at Latimer as he said it. Latimer remained silent and expressionless.

"True, but... major countries stopped using CFC's and other pollutants as early as nineteen eighty. Third world countries however, did not. Worse, substitutes for freon based refrigerants weren't invented until near the end of the century. As a result, two hundred and fifty million tons of chemical junk was dumped into the atmosphere between the early nineteen hundreds and two thousand and eleven. Most of it will still be with us for another hundred years, or so."

"A hundred years?" the President questioned. "That is somewhat difficult to accept."

"But true, nevertheless," Jill stated, reaffirming her presence. Although she looked at him this time when she spoke, she kept her gaze on the small cleft in the President's chin rather than honor him with a direct look into the haughty eyes. The cold, thin slice of a mouth was equally bad while the nose was laced with the fine blue lines of blood vessels normally attributed to excessive alcoholic consumption. Thus she had compromised on the chin as a point of reference. And then, when she finally looked away she caught Sam's eyes. He gave her a hint of a smile and a short wink that said, Good girl. Nice going.

"Can you elaborate on the specifics of the problem the

reflectors created?" Stein asked, without directing the question directly to either Jill or Korsak, playing the diplomat.

Sam watched and smiled as Jill and Korsak exchanged glances once more. Again, she nodded approval to Korsak, letting the group know that she was still the person who was really in charge.

"The aluminized plastic reflectors are not one hundred percent efficient, as you know. They absorb a small percentage of the radiation, creating a warm boundary layer at the surface. They also polarize light at the ultraviolet end of the spectrum. The combined effect causes chlorine to be liberated from the existing pollutants still in the air. A significant portion of this chlorine finds its way into the stratosphere. And, you know what happens at that point," Korsak stated.

"Yes. But what about the molecular recombination and Sarin gas production? How does that occur?"

"It might be best if Dr. Kairns explained that part," Korsak said, playing the game some more.

Jill hesitated for a moment, shot the President a direct look for effect, turned back to Stein and began.

"The predominant mechanism is the ultraviolet. Both in the upper atmosphere due to the non existent ozone layer and polarization at ground level which not only liberates chlorine but also alters certain hydrocarbons, photophenolyns and other organic derivatives, freeing them to recombine in ways that are extremely harmful to almost all life forms on the planet.

"Are you trying to say that we have to remove the reflectors?" the President said, his eyes narrowing.

"Not necessarily."

"What does that mean?" the President turned to Korsak and asked.

"There is an alternate, more expedient way to solve the problem. That's why we suggested that General Barnes be present. It's vitally important to do it quickly and it's going to take a lot of manpower."

"Obviously," Barnes said. "Except that it sounds more like something the Army Corps of Engineers should be undertaking. Unless you're suggesting we drop bombs on all of them, the Air Force has a mission different than disassembling physical structures."

"I agree," said the President. "And while the Unites States may have provided most of the money for putting them up, there is no way in hell we can expect the taxpayers to foot the bill for tearing them down. Those other countries will just have to take care of themselves on this one, regardless of what approach is taken. Besides, shouldn't we be building more ozone generators?" the President asked, looking directly at Jill, as if the entire catastrophe was her own personal fault. "I understand that at least they work."

"Yes, they do," she said, trying to maintain some neutrality in her voice, "but with the present trend it's analogous to trying to empty the ocean with a bucket. A very small bucket."

The President accepted the statement in silence and the room was still.

During all this time Sam had continued to stay out of the discussion, since it seemed clear that none of them would be willing to recognize him as any kind of authority figure. Nor did he enter the discussion when Barnes finally asked what the alternate to tearing the reflectors down might be. Korsak chuckled and said that while bombing them might be very effective it wouldn't have to come to that and then explained Sam's idea of simply spraying or dropping paint on them.

There was another moment of silence before Dr. Stein then asked,

"What do you propose we do after we remove the reflectors? We still need to get the planet cooled down."

"I'm not sure we know at this time," Jill said.

"What about a dust cloud in the upper atmosphere. Isn't that what the former head of your organization kept proposing?" asked Barnes.

"Doctor Rouard? Yes, but it's extremely risky."

"What's risky about dust?"

"As you may recall, General, it was the similar threat of so called 'nuclear winter' that finally forced our countries to modify their approaches to weaponry," Korsak pointed out.

"But it would cool down the planet. Isn't that right?"

"Without a doubt."

"Then why not do it?"

"It's been a very controversial subject. Dr. Rouard felt clouds of dust could be stabilized over the oceans and unpopulated areas but the general consensus of opinion is that such clouds would migrate regardless, devastating other areas before it eventually precipitated out."

"How fast would the clouds drift?"

"It's difficult to tell exactly. A matter of months, probably."

"But you could predict the cloud paths, couldn't you?"

"Maybe up to a point, once they began to move, however..."

"So why not move our agriculture around to where the sun gets through?"

"We don't have enough good land as it is, what with the present weather conditions. Not in this country at least."

"Well. That's certainly easy enough to fix," the general stated but before he could elaborate the President stood up, looked at Korsak, said thank you for coming, indicated to the rest of his people that the meeting was over and asked Dr. Stein to escort the visitors out of the building. After they were gone the President dismissed the general with a reprimand. Keep his personal views to himself or face some discipline.

"I still think you should have let me and Burkey handle this and not attended the meeting yourself," Latimer said as soon as the door was shut behind the general.

"I need to know what's going on, Arnold. First hand," the President said as he sat back down.

"Yes, but not with that reporter in there," he said and reached for his pack of cigarillos. "Who knows what he will make of it."

"Could you not light that in here?"

Latimer replaced the thin brown stick of tobacco back in the pack as the President continued.

"If he writes about this meeting he goes to jail but right now we have bigger things to think of."

"Are you really going to do what they suggested and take the reflectors down?"

"Of course. At least here in our own country where we are going to make it look like we take the matter seriously. Whether we actually do something elsewhere is unimportant as long as we buy a little more time."

"Understood."

So how is our unknowing good friend Dr. Rouard doing?"

"On schedule. I'll be talking to Burkey in Iran tonight for an update."

"Well, personally, I don't have a lot of confidence in that nincompoop. What if he isn't able to make it work? If his mission fails, the ozone problem will also become a northern hemisphere problem and we don't want that, do we?"

Latimer was quiet for a moment. "I still didn't like that reporter sitting in," he said.

"It's not him I'm worried about. If we play it right he might turn out to be our biggest helper. It's the General. The stupid ass doesn't even know it but he's giving half the plan away. Maybe we should have let him in on it in the beginning."

"No, but maybe you should consider an early retirement for him. Effective immediately. And what about Gorhman? What were you thinking?"

"As soon as the clouds are in place the Arabs will take care of Rouard and our own private task force will in turn eradicate all direct connections to the Arabs. Am I correct."

"Yes, sir. When we're done it will look as if the Arabs acted completely on their own."

"Just like it already does in Russia and South America. And who better to write the story that will expose the Arabs than that very reporter who was just sitting out there in our own conference room?"

TWENTY FOUR

The television was on in Jill's apartment. Coverage of street fighting in South America that had occurred earlier was being aired on the flat wall screen.

"Buenos Aires fell to the revolutionaries late last night. President Garcia fled southward to Tres Puntas where the new capital has been established. Garcia once again blamed the United States for failing to come to his countries aid," the announcer said as footage showed Garcia getting off a military jet in his new, forced upon location.

The announcer continued. "There was also further tragedy in Jabopol, India this morning as nearly two thousand members of the New Church of the Revelation jumped to their deaths."

The screen showed a steep, rocky cliff that dropped nearly two hundred feet to the river below. The river banks were strewn with the bodies of hundreds of men, women and children as seen from both above.

"Nearly the entire town of Jabopol and much of the surrounding area had recently been converted to the new faith by missionaries from the middle east. The citizenry were said to be disgruntled over a claimed failure of the United Nations Emergency Relief Organization to supply food and medical supplies," the announcer continued as the camera moved to a long row of buildings and then inside. "Government officials, however, found a total of nine tons of wheat still in sacks in warehouses near the center of town. An investigation is underway."

"In central Brazil the reforestation program has had serious setbacks due to unseasonably heavy rains that have washed most of the new seedlings away."

"Lightening has caused a series of forests fires in Siberia which are burning out of control. Approximately forty thousand square kilometers of timber are in jeopardy."

"On the up side, the new hydroponics farm in Northern England will begin harvesting it's first vegetable crop next week. This will come as a tremendous relief to Britons who have faced a severe shortage of..."

Sam rose from where he had been sitting on the couch with Jill and shut it off.

"Sorry," he said. "I can't stand to watch it any longer," and went back to her side. He put his arm around her, pulled her near and began kissing her ear.

"This is far more pleasant," he said and moved down to her neck.

"Keep going," she replied. "You're headed in the right direction."

It was just then that the phone rang.

"Hello," Jill said, when she picked it up from the nearby table. "Just a minute."

"It's for you," she said as Sam leaned over and reached for the phone while he also ran his free hand up the inside of Jill's leg and grinned at her.

"Jesus Christ. You're a hard one to track down," the voice of Bill Grisson boomed out from the instrument. "Who's the lady?"

"Jill Kairns."

"You mean that blond intellectual you were telling me about? Dr. Kairns, that is."

"You got it."

"Hope I didn't interrupt anything."

"You did and you know it. Anyway, what's up Bill, run out of ink?"

"No, but I could use another good story. And maybe I've got one you can pull together."

"How so?"

"Got a late call last night. No name. Some guy wants to meet you privately. Claims to know what happened to your friend Jed and wants to expose something that's going on."

"Think it's on the level."

"The guy sounded straight enough to me."

"Interesting."

"Sure is."

"How do I reach him?"

"You don't. But since I was pretty sure you were somewhere in New York I told him I'd try to find you."

"Is he going to call you back?"

"No. He said if I caught up to you I should have you come around to the Peking House over on thirty second around nine. He's seen your picture somewhere and would pick you out."

"You mean tonight?"

"Yeah, tonight."

"It's already eight thirty."

"I know, but if you can't make it or I was unable to reach you, he will call me tomorrow with another meeting place."

"Okay. But first let me see if I can get there in time. Thanks Bill."

"Hey, good luck. But watch your backside, goddammit."

Three hours later Sam let himself back into Jill's apartment. He watched Jill lying there sleeping, her golden hair spread out across the pillow, undressed quietly and tried to snuggle up without disturbing her. She stirred, however, and mumbled something. He kissed her lightly on the cheek and she turned and smiled a, half awake, smile.

"More, please," she said sleepily, and reached for him.

Tenderly he kissed her, when suddenly she sat up.

"Tell me what happened."

"Now?"

"Yes, now. I was worried about you. Tell me. Who was this person?"

"Some middle aged guy from inside the National Security Agency. Nameless, of course."

"Of course."

"I know, but bottom line, although I didn't get any new information, I got something just as important. He confirmed our worst suspicions."

"About what? That our findings were correct? What could be worse than that?"

"It was deliberate."

"You mean...?"

"Yes. The entire thing, manipulated right from the beginning. Some dark program called Grey Sky. It sounds pretty bizarre but as we already know, someone in the government didn't want your discovery known. They suspected, or, already knew what was happening to the atmosphere and merely kept funding UNACC, and consequently you, through UNACC, simply to confirm it. And, since it was a southern hemisphere problem, they purposely weren't going to do anything about it and didn't want the public stirred up over it."

"What are you saying? That it was all a farce, that I was being used?"

"You, Rouard, all of it. Their simple minded intent was to just let the ozone depletion effect wipe out most of the people of Africa and Australia. The fewer the people in the world, the better their own chances of survival."

"That's ghastly and stupid. As if the effect would be limited to that part of the world alone."

"Yes, but there's more. They had, or have, a backup scheme of some sort to hasten and insure the end of the southern hemisphere population should the ozone problem not be as severe as they thought, or if the public forced the administration to try and do something about it before they were ready."

"What could it be?"

"He's trying to come up with more information. And I know you liked the old bastard but somehow I feel Rouard is involved."

"Is that what this person told you?"

"No. That's me talking."

"That doesn't seem possible."

"How long has it been since you've seen or heard from him, two or three months?"

"Yes. Maybe more."

"What's he been doing all this time?"

Jill sat cradling her cup in her hands, staring into the pale liquid. "I hope he has more pride than that because it could only mean one thing."

"High altitude dust clouds?"

"Yes."

"I'm sorry," Sam said.

"Do you think a story about that would help if it got out in time?"

"There is always some public reaction, but..."

"But you're skeptical."

"Unfortunately, yes," Sam said. "Look what happened after your discovery hit the news."

"What do you mean?"

"I was in a bar having a drink when the networks picked it up. Know what the guy sitting next to me said? He said, what bullshit. Just another scare story so they've got another excuse to raise our goddamned taxes. And the guy next to him - he says, big fucking deal. A little more sunlight coming through ain't gonna hurt the Africans. That's what they have black skin for."

"But that's only two people, Sam."

"Sure, but there was no great public reaction, either. No overwhelming demand for action, no request for more information, no large query about what to do or how to help. Apathy, just brain dead apathy, for the most part."

"Some of it I can understand."

"Sure, me too. It's a complicated problem. Makes the average person feel pretty helpless, to be sure. Plus the fact that it's been a long, dismal, depressing last few years. Mass starvations, disease, severe climate changes, massive property damage. No end in sight to any of it, either, and all the while some nations are still waging war against each other. It's an insane time and getting worse."

"So you really can't blame the people."

"No. And I guess if I was some average guy struggling along I'd probably just get drunk and stay drunk until it was over, good or bad."

"I know. I was feeling the same way when I walked out of my meeting the other day, but..." Jill said as she got up, came over to where he sat and straddled him, her face in his face. "not too drunk. That might interfere with something else."

The next day when the phone rang Sam thought it was

Bill calling him back but to his surprise it was his former employer, old Hudson Soloman himself, owner of the Los Angeles Mirror.

"Don't hang up, Sam," Hudson said first thing.

"Why not?" Sam wanted to know, considering the circumstances under which he left.

"Because I have something that's right up your alley. And since your freelance now, I can pay you very well for it."

"What's wrong with Cliff?"

"I put the dumb shit in the accounting department, out of the way. You'd be doing it directly for me."

"What's it about?"

"There have been some mysterious night missile launchings from a small island in the South Indian Ocean with strange comings and goings that looked like the Arabs were involved and a report that the former head of UNACC, Dr. Rouard has been seen in the area."

What kind of a coincidence was this, Sam wondered to himself. Was it possible?

"Where did you get the information?" he asked.

"I have a contact in the intelligence community."

"That's very interesting," Sam stated. "What branch?"

"Foreign. From Europe."

"How do you know he's bona fide?"

"It's a she, and I've known her for years."

Very strange, Sam decided. Two people out telling stories, stories that appeared to interlock with each other. Why? Did someone think he was that stupid? He asked more questions. If Hudson had the answers, he evaded them cleverly. "When can you leave," Hudson asked him instead.

TWENTY FIVE

"Bud," she said, barely able to hear above the traffic noise and the bad connection the borrowed cell phone had as she stood out in front of a small, run down market. The thermometer on the bank building across the way registered one hundred and eleven. The sun on her back felt even hotter as it burned through the thin blouse she was wearing.

"Jean? Is that you?"

"Yes."

"Where are you? What's wrong?"

"Nothing's wrong Bud. I'm okay. I'm in Needles."

"California? What are you doing there?"

"Waiting for the bus to L.A.. It gets in around midnight. Then the Malibu bus leaves there at six forty in the morning so I should be in Santa Barbara by nine thirty tomorrow."

"How did you get to Needles?"

"A friend of Dawn's gave me a ride."

"Why didn't you wait till next weekend. My boss said I could borrow his car."

"I can't wait, Bud. I just want to be with you."

"I know, honey, and I want to be with you. But don't take the Santa Barbara bus. I'll come down and get you in Los Angeles. Wait for me if I'm late."

"Why, Bud? I'll be all right."

"No. It's much too dangerous. I don't want you spending the night in the bus station. If I can't borrow a car. I'll hitch hike and we'll take the bus together in the morning."

"Are you sure? You don't have to."

"I'll be there."

"You're not mad at me, are you?"

"I miss you too much for that."

It never gets totally dark in Los Angeles at night, even in the outer reaches of the city. There are few stars to be seen, either, even during the dark of the moon, because they are much too dim to compete with the all pervading sky glow that hangs over the entire basin, scattering its dim, errant light into corners and windows, diluting the darkness, creating only half shadows that deprive the ugliness of a true place to hide. The city never totally sleeps, either, so there is always someone out there viewing it, becoming a part of it, breathing the lung eroding air, exposed to the whine and the din and the screech and the screams in the night. Pick a corner.

The freeways are even worse, the ones still in operation after the monster earthquake of two thousand nineteen. Lane after lane crammed with vehicles all adding to the ruckus and the roar and the stench and the ugliness. Endless rivers of lights flowing in and out, and through and across, carrying an uncertain and devious cargo of goods and humanity from where to who knows where. Yes, where?

"Where are they all going at this time of night?" Jean asked, as they got off the surface streets and onto the detour route around the still devastated downtown area.

"I wonder if half of them even know," Bud said.

"I had no idea it would be so depressing. It looks as if they fought the war of the worlds here."

"Wait until you see it in the daytime."

"Why haven't they tried to rebuild, or at least clean it up?"

"From what I hear, the cost to clean it up is now more than the land is worth. Much of the later construction was heavily financed so the owners just walked away from their loans. With no demand for repossessed rubble piles, many of the lenders failed, also. The City Council tried to push through a bond issue but the people voted it down. Then they tried to raise taxes and there was a real revolt. It's a hopeless tangle that may take years to unravel. And now, with everything else that's going on in the world, nobody cares anymore. So they fenced it in and gave it over to anyone brave enough to live there."

"How big was the quake? I forgot."

"An eight point seven."

"Wasn't that the one triggered by underground testing? What were they doing that for?"

"Looking for more oil. That, and all the oil already pumped out of the ground under the city over the years. There were some huge holes down there. Together, it created some unusual stress patterns along the fault lines."

Jean shuddered and moved closer to Bud as he fought his way through the still dense traffic of the bypass and tried to pull her attention back inward but soon found herself staring off into the never-never land of destruction.

"There are bon fires in there," she said, "and I can see people."

"I know."

"How much farther until we are past?"

"Another mile, maybe."

Jean sat silent and brooding. "Are you all right?" Bud asked, once they were past the worst of it.

"What... Oh, yes," she said, shaking off the feeling. "I'm sure glad you came down and picked me up."

"Now you understand why I couldn't leave you in the bus station alone."

He put his arm around her and drove with one hand. Jean kissed his cheek and put her hand on his upper leg. Bud pulled her closer and let his free hand find it's way down inside her blouse. After they cleared the central city and got into the less congested north bound route, Jean began to tease him in earnest. Impulsively, Bud left the freeway in Agoura Hills and parked on a side road. He did it once again near Ventura. What should have been a two hour trip had become four. When they finally stumbled into the mobil home Bud had rented just south of Santa Barbara, they happily and heavily reeked of sex and no longer needed the lights to find their way in the first gray light of a new day.

"It's wonderful, Bud," Jean said as he showed her their diminutive new home. It had been a long separation for the two of them. After a quick shower together, Bud set the alarm and they managed to get three hours sleep before it went off. Although he told her to stay in bed, Jean insisted on getting up.

"What do you eat?" she wanted to know after inspecting the almost empty cupboards and refrigerator.

"I skip breakfast, have lunch in the cafeteria at work and stop someplace on the way home. No problem."

She just looked at him, shook her head and wondered how far it was to the grocery store but asked him how far it was to where he worked, instead.

"About five miles."

"But if that's your bosses car, how do you get there? I hope you don't have to walk."

"No," he laughed. "I bought an old motorcycle. Doesn't look like much, but it runs."

Jean had never pictured Bud on a motorcycle before. It took a moment to adjust. "Will it hold two people?" she asked, also trying to visualize herself on the back.

"It's a full sized bike, if you're up to it."

"I'd feel more comfortable if it ate hay and I could put a saddle on it but I guess I'll manage. Where is it?"

"I left it at work so I could bring the car home," he said, tucking in his shirt tail before bending over to tie his shoes. Straightening up, he went to her and put his arms around her.

"This isn't exactly the Ritz but I'm damned glad you're home, he told her for what must have been at least the tenth time.

"Me, too," she said, as they held each other.

"I forgot to ask," Bud said. "How are your parents?"

She shrugged and was silent.

"What's wrong?"

"My father," she said sadly. "He's in the hospital. I think he's dying."

"How long has he been there?"

"Two weeks."

"Why didn't you tell me?"

"I thought you had enough to worry about with your new job and finding a place to live, and everything."

"What do you think we should do?"

"We can talk about it tonight when you get home."

"I can stay a little longer."

"No, I'm okay, and I know you are late. Come on, I'll walk you outside."

At the car Bud said, "I'll pick something up on the way home. Pizza or hamburgers?"

"Neither. Just come straight home."

"But there's nothing in the house except some fruit and a

box of crackers. I'm sorry."

"Don't worry," she said, and kissed him good-bye. "I'll figure something out."

"How did you mange this?" Bud asked when he sat down for dinner.

"I made friends with the lady next door and we spent the day looking for groceries."

"I'm impressed. What with all the hoarding going on."

"This is all fresh. There isn't a thing that comes in a can left in town. No dried foods, either. Or bottled items or packaged goods. Anything that can be stored. Although we did find some coffee, sugar and flour. I also had my hands on some canned pears for about five minutes."

"What happened?"

"Some nasty bitch ripped them out of my arms. If her husband hadn't been so damn big, I would have decked her."

Bud laughed, knowing it was true.

"If I can find some mason jars," Jean continued. "I'm going to start canning again. And please eat. I want you to keep your strength up because I have other plans for you than just work."

They ate quietly, sitting at the tiny, fold down table decorated with a borrowed white cloth and a single, long tapered candle which illuminated the high points of each other's faces as they stared back and forth, each thinking how beautiful the other looked. Their unity was now completely intact, they felt whole again. Later they talked about her father and then he told her about his job.

"I'm probably the most over qualified, under paid person in the place. But, no complaints."

"You don't sound too happy."

"No, but I'm learning a lot."

"What's the rest of it?"

"Politics, waste and stupidity. Politics got me the job because I knew David from college but politics could take it away. The supervisor in the next section is pissed because I got

137

the job instead of his friend, so he gives me a bad time. The group leader is a brother in law of the section head and the operations manager is the brother of the US Senator from California. And even with those eminent connections, the place is still run from Washington, since it is entirely government funded. Almost the whole of Congress has been through the place in the last month."

"What for?"

"Pre election politics. It's an experimental facility and it's beginning to produce some spectacular results even though we spend more time giving guided tours than we do working, and generate more paperwork than vegetables. Regardless, even if it's only mildly successful, everyone will want a part of the credit. They'll also want similar facilities in their own states."

"How productive is it?"

"Potentially, one small, fifteen by thirty five foot greenhouse with artificially assisted illumination will yield about the same amount as a full acre of fertile ground. And, even better, do it three or four times a year, depending on the type of crop."

"What kind of yields are they getting now?"

"Between what the visiting dignitaries take with them and what the employees eat or steal, it's hard to tell exactly."

"What happens to the rest?"

"It's either analyzed to death or it goes in the trash. Regulations. Even the welfare groups can't have it."

"What a pity. Why isn't private enterprise getting involved? It should certainly be profitable enough."

"And it would be, if it could be done on a large enough scale. But the last company that tried it ran into trouble with the farm labor unions. First they picketed it, then they tried to burn it down and then they ended up poisoning the water supply."

"That's insane."

"No more than the midwestern farmers who drove live hogs into bulldozed trenches and killed them by the hundreds just because the government wouldn't increase their price supports."

"It's still insane."

"Of course it is. Doesn't make a person fell very hopeful, sometimes. Maybe we should be looking for a small piece of land ourselves. Start our own hydroponics and begin canning the surplus like you suggested."

"Why aren't we just rich? We could lay in a ten year supply and not have to worry about it."

"Which is what many of the rich are already trying to do. But, if it comes to that, I wouldn't trade places with them."

"Why not?"

"If the system collapses, currency will be worthless and the rich will have lost their power. They won't be able to purchase goods and services any more than anyone else and will be forced to barter their stockpiles to get what else they need. Once the rest of the starving people find they have food, guess what? No matter how high the walls around their estates, the mob will attack like a bunch of rabid rats. Frankly, I'd rather have a much lower profile and take my chances elsewhere."

"Sounds like you've been doing some thinking."

"It was all those nights alone without you."

"Funny. I was doing the same thing."

"And what did you come up with?"

"I think we should either start a survival group or be prepared to make our way back to Arizona and be with Dawn and Trent. They have one. In fact, many of the Indian clans have already made most of their own preparations. They have caches of food and supplies scattered over wide ranges of the state in remote places that are only accessible on foot. If it gets really bad, their idea is to split into a number of independent, nomadic bands, all self supporting. They also feel that while the first few months are critical, the bigger problems will come later."

"Why?"

"It's hard to believe that under extreme conditions even the police or the military would be able to maintain order over so many people. If they are starving, they will panic and become violent. The strong and the dangerous will be in

139

control. The rest will be dead within a month or two from starvation or disease. Within a few more months the rest of the survivors will be at war with each other over any remaining stockpiles of food. Then, the survivors of that conflict will be even more dangerous and as their supplies are used up they will have to leave the city to save their own necks. Thus the necessity of small groups of people living in isolation away from towns until that segment has also perished or destroyed each other."

"But it could last for years. And I think it would be very difficult to stay out of sight."

"Perhaps, but they are all relearning the use of knives, bows and arrows, traps and snares, tracking and all the old skills. No guns. Just silent ways to hunt and protect themselves."

"And to think that some of the people at work still sit around and talk about ways to flaunt their money. New car, bigger house, more clothes. I don't understand it."

"Reality is hard to face. And sometimes the closer it gets to crisis, they harder they work to avoid the real truth."

"But fortunately, they are not all that way. My friend David is a very decent person and so is his wife. And then there's a guy in Administration who wants us to come over. Also the doctor who gave me my physical. I almost forgot. He wanted me to call as soon as you got here."

"Really? What for?"

"After I told him we both had credentials in the area of agriculture and animal husbandry he said he wants us to come down and meet his wife. She's a psychologist."

"Seems a bit unusual," Jean said as the conversation slowed.

"Yes. Just like you are. You have no idea how glad I am that you took the initiative and came ahead of time. I sure missed you."

"Thank you," she said in return. "But there's one thing I need to know."

"What's that?"

"Well, the bed squeaks and the walls are thin just like

140

back in Chicago. Do you think the neighbors will be able to hear us?"

"Do you care?"

"What do you think?"

TWENTY SIX

How had they ever located this lost and desolate place, Rouard wondered as he stood looking out to sea in the wee, wee hours of the morning, wishing he had a boat or a raft or even that he had the ability to swim somewhere. Anything, so he wouldn't have to climb inside that cramped, stifling little capsule and take that awesome, frightful ride upward with that obsequious Swatch and that beady eyed, malevolent Arab into the higher reaches of that sparse, near void he had spent half a lifetime studying.

But it was hopeless. He was trapped and there was no escape. With the shoreline of the nearest continent at least a thousand miles away, he was now the hapless, helpless victim of all the preceding moments of his life which had led him here. There had been many choices along the way, other paths and other alternatives, now all suddenly reduced to none. And, good Christ. Even his last meal here was a disgrace. Stringy, over cooked lamb stuffed inside a stale half of pita bread and a can of American beer, all as course and crude as the people he had been surrounded by of late. It was all so damned hostile. Even the island, there in the light of the quarter moon, full of rocks and thorny plants and misshapen trees that literally defied you to come near.

Well, at least the wind wasn't blowing at the moment. There was hardly even a breeze, thank god, no rustle in the trees. Even the surf was down and the only viable sound that came through was the muffle of voices behind him, farther back towards the center of the land blob he stood on.

He turned and stared back in the direction of the voices and looked once again at the long, shiny, tapered profile of the missile pointing upward into the night sky, its capsule waiting for the human cargo it would soon carry aloft. Him. And

141

Swatch and that other sinister one who had only arrived on the island two days ago. God help him but he would be glad when it was over. Thinking about it, he began to sweat again. Too bad there wasn't time for another cold shower. But it was out of the question. He'd better get going or they'd come looking for him.

Liftoff would be the worst, he suspected. And until they had the space shuttle in their possession he'd have to wear that damned suit and helmet. Being more than slightly claustrophobic, that was the part that bothered him the most.

Still, it was to be a short mission, six or seven hours at most and then they'd be down. Twelve hours after that he'd be in Tehran collecting all that beautiful money and then he'd be free. Forever free to do what he chose. But god damn, if only it were over. If only he could keep his heart from beating so loudly, if only he could stop sweating, if only...

The liftoff was flawless. Except for the feeling that the tissues of his face were being torn off during the earlier moments of the vertical portion of the ride, it was relatively pleasant. There was none of that bone rattling vibration so characteristic of the older liquid fueled rockets he'd heard so much about and dreaded so fearfully.

The newly developed, controllable burn rate, solid fuel engine was smooth as silk and gentle as a new Rolls. American made, however. And a powerful son-of-a-bitch too, allowing an east to west launch trajectory, fighting the natural forces of the earth instead of taking advantage of the eastward kick due to the spin of the globe on its axis. Difficult, but more direct. Technologically marvelous, it would also be more confusing for anyone who happened to be awake on this side of the world at this hour. Again he wondered how the Arabs had managed to get their despicable paws on such a fine piece of obviously American made equipment.

Were they slowing? Rouard wondered. The force of the seat ramming into his backside had diminished considerably and his facial muscles began to relax. He watched Swatch lift his arms and begin to operate switches on the iridescent control panel. He tried to lift his own arm and succeeded relatively easy, then sensed the nose of the craft pitching slightly downward. There was another sound from deep in the craft below them. Must be the second stage letting go, he thought. Then he leaned towards the small viewing port and looked out. Blackness above, blackness below. He pushed closer. Then, out of the corner of his eye he saw it. Ahead, to the right of the craft, there was one portion of the earth heavily subdued in moonlight while behind them, the remainder of the full arc of the planet was illuminated by its rising sun. God it was beautiful.

Then the final separation from the last stage of the rocket occurred, right on schedule. Now it was just the tiny capsule with its three human occupants curving gracefully through the ultra thin upper reaches of the atmosphere in a mute, weightless silence that seemed to last forever. Finally it was interrupted by the occasional exterior gaseous hiss of the small attitude control thrusters making minor corrections to their trajectory.

"There it is," Swatch said at last.

"What," said Rouard, straining to see.

"The old Russian booster."

"I don't see it."

"On the radar screen," Swatch said harshly.

"Oh," Rouard replied, finally making it out.

Swatch began changing course, bringing the capsule around through a curving, miles long, one hundred and thirty degree turn and brought up their speed to overtake the booster. "Now you can see it out the window," Swatch said.

Rouard looked again. Yes, there it was, its gleaming aluminum bright in the moonlight, the hammer and sickle still as clear and visible as the day it was applied. Swatch slowed the capsule slightly and trimmed the velocity to correspond with the booster as he moved in under it.

"About ten more minutes," Swatch pointed out and began his final preparation.

Outside their capsule a sealed door opened and the gimbaled pointing mirror for the infrared laser inside the craft swung out to give it a free line of sight forward, along with the small microwave tracking sensor to which it was slaved. The sensor and mirror began a controlled raster scan of the void ahead and then stopped, locking onto it's target another hundred miles ahead, confirming the accomplishment by illuminating a green light on the control panel inside.

"We have acquired the space station communications dish," Swatch advised them and nudged the capsule in even closer to the booster, then sat quietly.

"Why don't you take it out?" Rouard asked.

"The laser beam divergence is too great to be effective at this distance," he said and watched the numbers on the digital range data display drop rapidly. When they were finally down to eight nautical miles he pushed the emit switch. Inside the bay of the capsule the long, optically folded, gas filled quartz tube glowed visibly red, generating a powerful source of much longer wavelength of invisible energy that poured forth and exited the silent mechanism. By means of a system of specially coated and precisely pointed mirrors, the fifty kilowatt beam of radiation was made to impinge directly onto the space station communications dish transducer, the most vital part of the link to earth. Within seconds the transducer began to glow red-orange. The red orange quickly turned to near pink and the pink to near white, rendering the complicated device completely useless, destroying the space station's ability to transmit or receive.

That accomplished, Swatch moved the pointing mirror to position the intense energy beam directly onto the skin of the central hub of the space station. Closer now and more concentrated, the invisible beam worked even faster, quickly heating the exterior wall of the station, burning through to the inner lining, cutting a line in the alloyed metal that grew to be a couple of feet long.

"Mon Dieu," Rouard said as the space station structure then fractured completely and exploded outward, carrying a shower of debris and human bodies through the gaping hole into the cold emptiness of space.

"Poor bastards," he said, finally realizing the horror of what he had become involved in.

Far below and much further to the west in Pretoria, South Africa, the African Chief of Staff had been lying in bed with the lamp on, reading a biography about General George Patton, reincarnated Napoleonic soldier, master of engagement and attack who commanded his last great battle some eighty years previous. He had finished the fourth chapter, put a scrap of paper in the book to serve as a marker, glanced at his wife asleep beside him and turned out the light. He had just begun to slide into the first episode of the nights dreaming when the phone rang, pulling him back to the place where walls cannot be walked through. His top staff assistance was on the line.

"Colonel Hascomb here, sir," the white man said to the black. "Our Cape Town observation site reports another missile launch and a much larger payload inserted into orbit."

"Cape Town? Not New Zealand? Explain."

"It originated from somewhere in the South Atlantic."

"A shipboard launch?"

"Much too big for that."

"What else is out there?"

"Not much. A few deserted islands is all."

"Is it headed in this direction?"

"No, sir. A rather unusual launch. Southeast to northwest."

"Southeast to northwest?"

"Confirmed, sir."

"...How long ago?"

"Fifteen minutes, perhaps."

"Fifteen minutes! Why wasn't I informed earlier?

"Maybe because of the launch direction? I just now arrived here myself...Hold a minute sir, we seem to have lost it."

"How could we loose it?"

"Space junk clutter. There's no end to it anymore."

145

The Chief listened as Hascomb moved the phone away and conversed with someone in the background. A moment later Hascomb spoke again.

"It's changed direction, now heading due east. It appears to have moved in near to, or rendezvoused with, some previously cataloged object going the same direction. They're checking now...It's an old Russian booster, very large, four meters diameter, eighteen meters long, been there for at least twenty years."

"Doubtful that it would be a rendezvous. What's the down orbit heading?"

"We're checking sir...South Atlantic, curving northward over Central America..."

"Isn't that the location of the American space station?"

"A...yes sir, it is."

"Mighty mysterious. What do you suppose those devious bastards are up to this time?" the Chief asked, but before Hascomb could respond he asked another question. "Can our high resolution scanners reach that far?"

"Pixel size would be about three or four feet at that range."

"Good enough. Follow that booster on around as far as we can see it and call me back in twenty minutes," the Chief said and hung up. Leaving the bedside lamp on, he gave his wife a reassuring pat and reached for his book.

Twenty minutes later he had the phone off the cradle before the first ring had completed. "Go ahead," he said.

"As you suspected sir. It diverted from the booster and rendezvoused with the space station. There was some initial activity we couldn't resolve but the object parked at the station and then the space shuttle moved off, back towards the east."

"Must be some new space game exercise the Americans dreamed up. Damned fools, they're still taking that star wars stuff too seriously. Too bad they don't have something else to do with their time and money."

"Yes sir."

"Well, keep a sharp eye on it and we'll give them a call in

the morning. Let them know we saw the whole damned thing. That ought to piss them off."

By the time they had concluded their conversation, the stolen space shuttle had proceeded to the previously parked canisters, loaded the two that would fit into the equipment bays, put the other under tow and began moving further east. Again the South Africans thought it was part of the same strange game the Americans were playing and failed to take it seriously as high above, Swatch gave instructions to Doctor Rouard.

"We will wait here until another dead booster casing comes around. Then we will hide in the shadow once more until we are back around to where the sun is setting. At that point we will drop down to the lower altitude you asked for to give your clouds more density and proceed in the direction of darkness to keep them unaware of our mission as long as possible. Make your final preparations. You have about twenty minutes."

Good, Rouard thought, that sounded logical, and began doing as he was told. Once completed there was time to spare and he sat looking down at the earth below, fascinated as he had never been in his whole life. White cloud formations were stirring around over the intense blue of the Pacific ocean. Here and there groups of islands were visible in the sunlight. There, that must be Tahiti, he decided. Their landing site. A couple more hours and they'd be there. Not so important anymore, he thought, surprising himself, now that they had made it up and his fear had finally subsided. Somehow he wished he could stay up there forever, away from the strife, looking down. It was so totally serene. Then, in the distance ahead, near the edge of the night time shadow he thought he could make out another land form.

"Four minutes Doctor," Swatch informed him.

Were they going that fast, Rouard wondered. They should just be approaching North Africa, not be past it already, but he said nothing. Three minutes later he swore he could see the

147

tops of the Andes mountains far ahead of them in the dim light. What was this? They weren't safely over the ocean, they were coming up on the west coast of Peru.

"Ready now," Swatch said. And then, before Rouard could respond, the final command. "Begin release."

"Are you mad?" Rouard said. "We're over South America."

Like a cat, the Arab, still to utter one word during the mission thus far, was out of his seat and at Rouard's side, having placed a wire noose around Rouard's neck.

"Do it now Doctor," Swatch said sharply, "or off comes your head. It's one of his specialties, you know. The wire is fine and sharp, quick and soundless. No thrashing about to disrupt anything."

Rouard stammered unintelligently.

"Decide, Doctor. Quickly."

Rouard's shaking hand reached for the controls in front of him as the noose loosened. Outside the craft the cargo bay doors swung open and the first canister of dust moved into position. The cover blew away as the inner mechanism began rotating, turning the hard packed powder to dust again and spewing it out in a long, dark trail.

Bastard's, he said to himself. They had tricked him, goddamn them. Where were they now? Only about five degrees south latitude if he was correct. The second orbit was further south and the third and final one even further, with Swatch increasing the vehicles speed with each orbit to keep the cloud densities approximately equal. Most of South America, the southern end of Africa, all of Australia, New Zealand, parts of Indonesia and all the south pacific islands were being sacrificed. What, a billion people at least? Yes, and more. But what could he do? Apparently nothing. At least if he wanted to go on living. And, obviously, even that wasn't guaranteed anymore.

"Well," he said, after reevaluating his position. "Why didn't they tell me what the real plan was. I could have helped automate the process somewhat."

"Don't worry, Doctor. We had already taken that precaution, just in case."

"Oh...I see. Well...Perhaps it's a better idea, doing the land masses as well as the oceans. Most of those people aren't going to make it anyway," he said, as if they might be spraying a wheat field, trying to rid it of a horde of locust. "This will just hurry it along a bit."

Swatch sat silently at the controls and ignored Rouard's chatter, leaving Rouard alone to deal with the awful thing he had taken part in, blanketing the entire southern hemisphere with dust, land and sea alike. But, so, what the hell. Maybe it really wasn't such a bad idea after all, he told himself as he lapsed into the usual line of bizarre rationalization he resorted to in moments of trauma, soon pushing aside all consideration for the moral incorrectness of his logic. It really wasn't so many people, actually. Not in terms of those already dead from the greenhouse effect and ozone problem thus far. And certainly not so many as compared to the ones still remaining. No, maybe it wasn't such a bad idea after all, except for the fact that they had forever ruined his chances for recognition in what would be left of the world. What would he do now? He'd be a hunted man for sure, once this deed had been discovered.

Before he could complete his thinking on the matter, however, the final canister had emptied itself and had been jettisoned. The cargo bay doors were closed and sealed. The nose of the vehicle began to pitch forward. They were coming in. Once on the ground they would soon know the effect the forming dust clouds would be having. Then Rouard would collect his money in Tehran and head north. Maybe Sweden. That might be far enough away.

Although they might have believed so, the South Africans weren't the only ones aware of the unusual night launches from the remote island in the South Indian Ocean. The American military was also quite aware of what went on but was prevented from sharing the information with the South Africans by presidential order.

Seemingly totally unrelated, they had also become aware of something else that had been happening half way around the world in the mid Pacific. Something which almost seemed too easy to have uncovered through eavesdropping on cell phone conversations taking place in Tehran and something relatively easy to confirm. It didn't matter that there was unusual activity going on under cover of darkness on that small island adjacent to Bora Bora, the advanced state-of-the-art satellite surveillance system made it all look sharp as day. Not that any of it was particularly alarming. It was just rather curious and peculiar. Especially since there was an airstrip involved.

"That's a very strange thing to do to a perfectly good landing field," Colonel Stevens said, as he showed the enlarged pictures of the island runway to General Simms as soon as they became available. "Especially after it seems to have been recently repaired."

"A little strange, to be sure. But I can't imagine what significance it might be. Still, it might give our men something to do. What part of the fleet is in the area?"

"The Hornet left the Marshalls yesterday on the way to Hawaii."

"Let's have it swing by and stand off shore for a few days. Run a flight or two over the island."

Unfortunately, the aircraft carrier was too late. At the same time it was also a little early. Too late to find anything on the island except the runway damage and an abandoned bulldozer and a little early for the unknown main event that would occur when the stolen space shuttle would attempt its landing. As for the final night launching they might have witnessed directly half a world away the night before on another equally small island, no connection was ever even considered. Except for the South Africans and a station in Argentina, it went unnoticed elsewhere due to the extreme southerly point of origination. The South Africans had automatically attributed it to the Americans, however, and the Argentinean intelligence officer who had noticed it, hadn't bother to report it. What point? His country was in such a state of disarray he wasn't sure who would be interested. As for the White House, a call came in from Latimer, after Latimer had gotten his coded message from Massad in the Middle East.

A White House Aide relayed an oddly worded message to the President. "Mr. Latimer says he will be staying in town tonight because it has been raining down south."

The President barely looked up from what he was doing. He simply nodded and noted the time. Right on schedule. Of course there was no way to tell how the engagement with the space station went. They could only wait. In the meantime he was glad that General Simms had taken the initiative and gotten the Navy to send the Hornet to Tahiti without his presidential involvement.

Fortunately, for the success of Rouard's mission, neither the Pentagon nor NASA headquarters at Langley were immediately aware of the events that took place at the space station. Having had the capsule hidden under the Russian booster had worked well because the western hemisphere monitoring radar stations had not been able to discriminate between the two objects when they passed over.

It had also been more than an hour later when the stolen shuttle was well into its first pass before any concern was raised. The Texas tracking station had detected its movement and when the autocorrelator had given a probable indication of what it was, NASA was informed. NASA then tried to raise the sleeping space station and then the shuttle itself, to find out what unscheduled venture it was being used for. When this failed, they contacted the smaller North Pacific platform and had them run their interstation shuttlecraft by to take a look.

"Why in hell would anyone kill a dozen men just to steal a ten year old shuttle craft?" General Simms wanted to know as he spoke to Davis at NASA.

"It's much more serious than that."

"How so?"

"They are using the vehicle to lay down what appears to be a rapidly dispersing, fine grained dust cloud over most of

151

the southern hemisphere."

"That's a little weird. But what's so serious about it?"

"I'd say someone is trying to fix the greenhouse effect by eradicating the entire population south of the equator."

Simms had to think about the statement for a moment before he realized what Davis meant. "You mean like the nuclear winter effect? The dust shuts out a portion of the sunlight producing a drop in earth temperature."

"Exactly, but if the density of the cloud is heavy enough, it will put an end to agriculture."

"More starvation. Will it work?"

"It depends on the size of the dust particles, how widely they disperse and how long they stay up there. Undoubtedly it will have serious consequences for most of Africa and the Australians."

"Holy Christ. Where is the shuttle now?"

"Second orbit completed and into the third."

"Talk to you later," Simms said. "I need to get downstairs."

Twenty seconds later Simms entered the high tech situation room with its elaborate back lit maps, charts and displays. A number of personnel were busy at various functions. He went directly to Colonel Stevens who was at a world map showing the ongoing plot of the shuttle craft's orbital position.

"What's their status?" Simms asked.

"They're nearing the end of the third orbit."

"Are they likely to continue."

"I wouldn't think so. The damage has been done."

An enlisted man at the nearest control station broke in. "It appears to have begun reentry sir," he said to the Colonel.

"What's the logical put down point?" General Simms asked.

"It looks like mid South Pacific, somewhere in the vicinity of Tahiti."

Suddenly it all came together for both Simms and Colonel Stevens, but Simms was the first one to say it. "Jesus Christ. Are those bastards in for a surprise," he said, thinking of the torn up runway near Bora Bora.

"Sir?" said the enlisted man, not understanding.

"Where's the Hornet?" Simms demanded.

"The Hornet, sir?"

"Our aircraft carrier."

Stevens made a quick input into the computer and a small orange light began to blink on the map.

"Right there, sir," he said. "Still standing offshore about ten miles from the island."

"Have her proceed immediately to get closer in. And get some helos ready to lift off. Then get me a direct link to the Admiral from my office," the General said and turned to go just as an alarm went off. He turned back to see flashing red lights emanating from northern Australia and working there way up in the direction of the shuttle trajectory.

"Australia has apparently launched defensive missiles. They're trying to shoot it down."

"Good grief. Can they reach it?"

"Highly unlikely. It's moving too fast and probably too far away."

Rouard could barely make out the eastern coast of Australia through the thin cloud cover and a portion of the Great Barrier Reef. Amazing. Was that a ship he could see? He thought so. Not long to go now.

Suddenly the craft underwent a severe jolt.

"What the hell was that?" he asked.

"I believe we are being shot at," Swatch replied.

"Shot at! Mon Dieu. What the hell is this?"

"The Australians must have panicked."

"Well do something, dammit. I don't want to die up here."

"Pray then, and shut up," he was told.

Down range the Hornet stood a quarter mile off shore. Half a dozen helicopters were on deck, full crews on board and rotors turning. From his privileged position in the upper reaches of the control tower, Sam Gorhman was witness to all that was going on. Old Hudson's contacts had been every bit as good as he had claimed. Too good, it seemed. There weren't any other media people on board at all. It was a glaring absence to Sam.

So far, however, it hadn't been much of a story, with little tangible evidence to tie whatever was going on to the Arabs. Just a small, abandoned island atoll with some recently used support equipment for missile launch and some scorched earth around a makeshift pad. Where will it lead, Sam wondered. Wherever it was, it wouldn't be good. The sky already had a strange, errie, dull glow off towards the west in the afternoon sun which was no longer completely visible. Damn. Hudson Solomon might be paying his way but Sam was already drawing his own conclusions on this one.

A highly amplified voice reverberated across the deck from the speakers on the control tower of the Hornet. "Shuttle touch down in ninety seconds. Prepare to go."

The deck crews retreated to the tower as the large drooping helicopter rotors picked up speed and flattened out, the deep, rapid, flump, flump, flump of the vanes rattling the entire vessel.

"Those goddamned sons-a-bitches," Swatch said loudly as they came gliding in from less than a mile off. "Hit the ejector," he shouted.

"What's wrong?" Rouard asked.

"Can't you see, for Christ's sake," Swatch said as reached over and hit a lever on the control panel, only to find that nothing happened. He pounded on it in frustration a few more times, then grabbed the wheel and began pulling frantically back with all his strength.

"Oh shit," Rouard said in French as a vision of his beloved Estelle flashed through his mind as the stolen space shuttle he was riding in crashed into and glanced off the coral shoreline and hit the water.

Immediately, two of the larger helicopters from the Hornet made passes over the floating craft and half a dozen frogmen dropped immediately into the sea with rubber lifeboats following swiftly behind them. It was a vain and useless gesture, however, because as they learned later, careening off the rocks had pierced the shell of the space craft and it sank like a stone in thirty feet of water, all of it, except for the upper portion of the vertical stabilizer that stood like a patriotic marker above the waves with its emblem of the American flag painted on it.

"At best, because of its low lift aerodynamic profile, landing the shuttle is somewhat analogous to making a high sink rate, controlled crash landing without power assist. The approach must be long and shallow with no chance of a go-around if you come up short. And while the runway was sabotaged, it was done in a very precise and regular fashion. The furrows were not that deep and the piles were located to disguise the trenches and blend with the asphalt. It would have been difficult to discern from a distance and by the time it was that obvious, it would have been too late to attempt a landing in the water instead." was the way the flight officer explained it to Sam.

"Why didn't someone try and warn them?"

"We did, but apparently they weren't listening."

Well, that was it. All they could do now was wait until the frogmen had gained entry into the submerged craft and checked for survivors, not that there was likely to be any. The carrier itself, had moved in as close to shore as possible and lay at anchor in the calm sea, less than two hundred yards away from the sunken hulk. Sam had been handed binoculars and was privileged to be plugged into the communications link with the divers working the scene.

A bright orange, inflatable rubber boat was tied to the dull, buff colored shuttle stabilizer jutting out of the turquoise water. One man was in the boat, two visible in the water, three somewhere in the depths below, all in black wet suits. Not too

155

far away, palm trees on the beach swayed slightly in the warm, benign, afternoon breeze. It was a most serene picture. Sam reached for his camera, snapped the long focal length lens in place, zoomed it out to about two hundred millimeters and started clicking the shutter as a voice came through the headset.

"Seaman Dugas here. I'm over the cabin windows."

"Can you see inside?"

"Yes, sir. Three occupants in the cabin. No one moving."

"Is the cabin flooded?"

"Only partially. There appears to be some seepage coming in from under the cabin floor."

"How much water?"

"Just a few inches so far."

"Okay, stand by. Carroll and Yates, how are you doing?"

"Ensign Carroll here. Yates and I have made entry. We are in the forward equipment bay just behind the cockpit module."

"What are conditions there?"

"It's almost fully flooded. We're trying to locate the manual release for the inter compartment door."

"Put a hold on that for now. Just in case any of them are still alive."

"Yes, sir. What instructions do you have?"

"Come back up for a bit. We're going to send the big helo over and put a line on it."

"Isn't the shuttle too heavy?"

"It is, if we try to bring it above water. But we'll use the chopper to drag it closer to ship side so we can get the deck winch on it."

"Acknowledged."

There were more instructions, more orders barked, giant rotor blades thumping the air, the whir of electric crane motors, the shouts above the noise. Sam clicked off a series of photos recording the major events of action as they occurred.

Two dead bodies were stretched out on deck, one was still inside the shuttle with the medics in attendance. Then the

156

report, "We lost him." Then there were three bodies on the deck. Rouard, who lived the longest, now lay alongside his unlikely compatriots, his bruised and bloodied face staring up at the premature dusk that had overtaken the southern world.

"Did he say anything," Sam asked the medics.

"He kept mumbling something about saving the world. At least that's what it sounded like."

"Vain to the last," Sam commented.

"Do you know this man?" the ship commander asked. "Who is he?"

"Dr. Pierre Rouard," Sam said somewhat scornfully. "Former head of the United Nations Atmospheric Control Council. God's gift to humanity. God bless us all."

"Why do you put it that way?"

"Look at the sky, Commander. Look at the sky."

"Instead of looking up the Commander pursed his lips and stared hard at the bodies before him. "Do you know the other two?"

"I've never seen them before."

"Any identification on them?" he asked of the medics.

"None, sir," the man replied. "The one looks American and the other is...middle eastern, I would guess."

"Well, get some body bags and get them in the cooler. We'll ship them back to the states first thing in the morning," the Commander ordered, then turned abruptly on his heel and headed back towards the control tower.

Sam stayed and watched the men work, staring at Rouard's face right up until the zipper closed it off from view. The ultimate in misdirection and madness, was all he could think of.

TWENTY SEVEN

"Yes Beverly," Jill said as she answered the phone that was ringing, after she had already given instructions to her secretary not to be disturbed. "What is it?"

"An urgent call from Australia, miss. The man said his name was Ernie. Do you want to take it?"

"Yes. Please put him on."

After a quick hello, she listened intently for nearly a minute. "Oh my god Ernie," she said. "Are you sure?"

"Yes," Ernie said. "It's still spreading out. Obviously it won't be a total obscuration but it most likely will scatter enough light to have a dire effect on both agriculture and ocean life."

"What do you think the cloud is composed of?"

"There's no way to tell as yet. Whatever it is, however, the particle size is very small because it's scattering primarily in the blue and green."

"Right at the peak of the solar spectrum."

"Yes."

"Do you have any of the converted high altitude missile probes left, or did we use them all?"

"I'll have to check," Ernie said. "And I'll get one ready if we do. Will you be coming home?"

"I'd like to. But I don't know. There's so much to be done."

"It would be nice to see you again."

"Thanks Ernie. You too. And Ernie...Do they know who did it yet?"

"Someone stole the American space shuttle and used it to lay down the dust cloud. Apparently the Americans just fished it out of the water off the coast of Tahiti where it crashed."

Jill was silent for a moment, thinking. "Were there any survivors?" she asked then. "Have they released any names?"

"They haven't made anything public as yet."

"Okay," she said, worried that Dr. Rouard might really have been involved somehow, as Sam had suggested before he had left so suddenly.

"Well, if we have a probe, send it up," she continued. "See if you can capture some samples of the material that was used to form the cloud. We will need to know. And if you need funds I can probably release some UNACC money."

With that, they said good-bye and Jill's thoughts turned back to Sam. Was he there when the shuttle had come down? Did he know the full story by now? And if he was right, what then? More than anything, she wished they were together.

"POSSIBLE ARAB INVOLVEMENT" Where in the hell had that come from? Sam asked himself, knowing full well what the answer was. They weren't his words, they were Hudson's, the son-of-a-bitch, words that had been added to Sam's story headlines with Sam's name as author at the top.

"Well, there was an Arab on board the shuttle when it came down, wasn't there?" Hudson had stated when Sam confronted him, trying to obscure his real reasons for implicating the Arabs.

"How can you incriminate them so readily?"

"They're guilty, all right," Hudson stated. "And we caught them with their pants down, the bastards, and the world needs to know about it," he said authoritatively, while inside he was thinking of them as "dumb" bastards. They'd be seething mad tonight.

"What about the pilot? He was American, for christsake, which somebody conveniently deleted from my story, goddammit. And Rouard, displaced Frenchman who's lived in half a dozen countries, most recently the US."

"I have other sources of information as I told you. I just can't reveal them yet. Why can't you let it go at that?"

"Because, not only is it totally irresponsible journalism, it's damned poor politics at a time like this. The world is a powder keg and you're trying to put a match to it. "What if it's another, under the table, CIA plot? Maybe even with the President's blessing? What then?"

"That's ludicrous and you know it," Hudson shouted at him, but not before his face paled.

"Yeah, and guess what I found out after I got back here?" Sam said in return. "Too late, of course, but I learned that you used to be buddies with the President way back in college days. How come that never came out before?"

"Because it has nothing to do with anything that's important, that's why."

"It has everything to do with a lot of things, now that I know what I know. But I'm glad I went. It gave me a first hand view of what some people will stoop to. Unfortunately, it may be too late even though it looks like your team won this round."

A pretty scheme it was too, Sam thought. One the Arabs would never be able to extract themselves from either, you could bet your ass on that. Because, sure as hell, there would a quick succession of follow on stories tying them to it every step of the way, burying them under world opinion before they could react and tell the rest of it. Unfortunately, however, by then no one would care about the truth. Especially in the US. Too bad about the southern hemisphere but don't worry folks, we're still safe here at home so what the hell. Get used to it and learn to take care of yourselves.

Cautious as Sam had been in the process, however, he had still been had, he realized. And that hurt. But, if he could somehow just make contact with his other mysterious stranger again, then he'd have a real story, maybe even the truth, now that he could see that this individual wasn't a part of the same conspiracy that Hudson was involved in. That side of the story would probably hang the whole administration out to dry. Goddamn them. The sons-a-bitches not only used Rouard, they had used all of UNACC, including Jill. And now they had used him. And for what? What was the real end game anyway? That was the really big question. The one he was now determined to find the answer to.

With that he scowled at Hudson and left the private office, walked past Hudson's personal secretary and went to the elevator. He needed to meet with Dr. Sheckman to discuss what progress had been made on their own private survival scheme and then make a stop at the marina before heading back to the airport. He could still make the five o'clock flight to New York. Above all, he wanted to see Jill again and then get to work on the story behind the story.

"How is the candidate list coming?" Sam asked Sheckman as soon as they had dispensed with the rest of it.

"We have a few good ones. Deanna has done comprehensive psychological profiles on them and they look compatible enough in such a situation"

"Who are they?"

"A young Chinese couple. He's an electronics engineer specializing in communications and she is a computer expert. I also found a jack of all trades contractor who's wife is a marine biologist, of all things. Then, I think I have a mechanical engineer lined up but I don't know if his wife has any useful skills. We'll also be talking to a young couple with agricultural and animal husbandry backgrounds.

The hull of the large sailing vessel Sam had acquired a few months earlier was now dull gray in color and did much to disguise her sleek lines, all ninety five feet of their sculptured fiberglass construction. Deck rails, hardware, water tanks, fuel tanks, everything possible that was made of metal had been stripped and replaced with composite graphite fiber, fiberglass, nylon or some other plastic substitute. The engine compartment, the cockpit and the galley had been lined with a special purpose absorbent material and the geometry changed in significant ways. All in all the vessel, when completed, would present an almost invisible appearance to even the best of marine radars and other sensor systems, military included.

Sam went on board and talked briefly with the crew chief before giving himself a tour. He was very pleased with the results. There were accommodations for fourteen, sail cloth for even the most benign of breezes, a two thousand gallons of diesel just in case, sonar, radar, GPS, solar desalinator, medical equipment and storage enough for a six months food supply. It might be a little cramped, perhaps, after it was fully stockpiled, but more than adequate. There was one advantage to troubled times, at least. Once very expensive toys like this were now quite cheap. Thank God because it was still costing him and Sheckman all their spare change. And if they never needed it? Well, there was still a lot of ocean out there beckoning, now that he had someone in his life he would like to share it with.

"Are you sure the President is involved?" Jill asked.

"Damned right," Sam said, back in New York.

"Then why has he asked for the meeting tomorrow to discuss proposals for removing the dust cloud from the stratosphere?"

"If you were involved, what would you do? What tactic would you use that would be most likely to convince people you were innocent?"

"But what if we have a viable approach that can be used?"

"No matter how good it is, it will still take time to implement. At that point he just lets the normal bureaucratic process take over and he can stall it indefinitely. Once the southern hemisphere countries are extinguished, then he can make an effort to clean things up if the cloud moves northward."

"It's...God, how could they even conceive of such a scheme? The man isn't human."

"Him and whoever else is involved. They're all insane."

"And it's not a question of, if it moves northward, but when, because it will do that, sooner or later, whether the administration realizes it, or not."

"All the more important why I have to find this mysterious stranger. Let's hope he's still alive."

"Yes. But even so, maybe I should go back to Australia and work with my own government. What do you think?"

"No, work with both, but stay here. This is the crucial spot. Come up with the best scheme you can. The simplest, most economical, least demanding thing you can think of and then push like hell to put it into effect. I can help, with the aid of Bill Grisson's newspaper. We'll follow the progress every step of the way, point out every bit of foot dragging, side stepping and deliberate bureaucratic blunder."

"I wish I could bring you to the meeting tomorrow but the White House staff was very adamant about it."

"Does that surprise you?"

"No. It only confirms what you say."

"But, it's okay. I'll be patient. We'll have our final

confrontation later. Hopefully, in full view of the public."

Jill tried to smile. "I'm sure you'll get your chance. If not, you'll make one."

Would he, Sam wondered. Would anyone, the way things were moving? He'd better hurry. If ever time was of the essence, it was now.

"Too bad you don't have a technical solution to propose as yet," he said. "Then we could really start putting on the pressure.

"I don't even have a glimmer of an idea."

"Between you and Korsak, you'll come up with something."

"By tomorrow?"

Sam's eyes had never left her the whole time they had been talking. "Sure. Why not. A giant space broom or vacuum cleaner or dust magnet or some such ungodly thing."

"Do you think so?"

"Dear, lovely lady, I know it."

TWENTY EIGHT

News of the dust cloud sent a new wave of fear and despair through the world that exceeded everything to date because it was also coupled with a deepening distrust of other people and other political systems, let alone lack of confidence in their own governments, whichever one it happened to be. Religious leaders had also failed dramatically in their efforts to provide meaningful answers during the prelude to the dust cloud. And, now that it was up there, they were even more at a loss. There was genuine desperation, growing daily as available food supplies began diminishing rapidly with increased hoarding and winter not that far off in the Northern Hemisphere. Looting and robbery were now common occurrences as armed guards became the order of the day for stores and warehouses and even farmer's fields. Elsewhere in the world there was mass murder committed by those in power in a last ditch effort to maintain order.

In South Africa even more monstrous forms of savagery

163

were to find their way to the surface, all quite unexpected by the Arab nations who suddenly found themselves surrounded by a sea of hatred. And although the news stories did not specifically delineate who was politically responsible for the dust cloud, the South African Intelligence Agency quickly traced Rouard's last movements to Tehran. That agency had also become aware of a newly formed secret coalition which included the neighboring countries of Syria, Jordan and North Saudi as well as Libya, Egypt, Turkey and Pakistan.

Unfortunately, knowing but a small portion of the facts can sometimes lead to drawing completely erroneous, unwarranted conclusions that have nothing to do with the real truth and such was the case here. The coalition was not imperialistic in any sense of the word. Instead, it was brought together to try and counteract all the blame that was being heaped upon the Arab nations in recent months. In spite of the fact that most of the middle east nations hated the western world in general and the meddling United States with particular passion, their goal was never to take up a military offensive against them. Being smarter than trying to start a war they could never win, their primary mission was to secretly get at the truth. The truth and the why of what began to happen three years earlier when the now American president first took office.

Thus, badly informed as they were, the military leaders of the nation of South African had still become aware that on this particular bland, late autumn day, the heads of state of those grossly unpopular countries had gathered in Tehran. Not to continue the madness but to undercover who amongst their midst had aided and abetted the Americans and to expose the United States as the real originators of the dust cloud cabal.

It was a heated discussion. Two of the leaders were already convinced of the Americans guilt in the matter and, contrary to their stated mission, were in favor of a direct assassination of the US President and the Vice President, the Secretary of State, Latimer and Burkey and a half dozen others. The personnel to do so were already in place in two different locations in downtown Washington DC. All it would take was coordination and timing to bring it about.

"No," declared the elected leader of the group. "First we must openly expose the Americans. It is the only sensible way. If we start exterminating them at this point we will only heap more hatred upon us."

"I would agree," said the Egyptian. "Place the blame first, kill them second. Then no one will care who was responsible for their deaths. In fact, the world would probably cheer us."

"And how would we do this?" was the next question.

"Start by kidnapping Latimer and Burkey. After a little drug therapy we will have enough details to build our case."

All in all, it might have evolved into a workable plan except for some otherwise minor details. A fresh grave had been dug up in the middle of the night in a small New Jersey town and a second body added to the one already there. That had taken care of Burkey. Latimer had just been picked up in a government limo and was en route to a similar fate in Maryland. The second item that would forever prevent the Arab plan from materializing, however, was yet to come. It had required a little more preparation.

TWENTY NINE

"Of all the places I never wanted to go to, Los Angeles is at the top of the list," Jill stated vehemently. "I'm sorry if it hurts your feelings, Sam, but I'd rather stay here."

"Doesn't hurt my feelings one bit. But it's not all bad, either," he told her.

"Name one good thing."

"Disneyland will soon be open gain."

She laughed, then sobered and asked, "Why do you really want to be there Sam? What's going on?"

He shrugged, not wanting to tell her just yet. Too much doom and gloom. Perhaps he had over exaggerated things to himself. Regardless, the state of affairs in the United States and abroad was rapidly deteriorating and deep in his gut he had a most wretched feeling.

"I'm a big girl, remember," she said. "And whatever is on your mind, I'd like to share it with you."

So he told her. About his worst fears, about the survival scheme of his and Sheckman's, about the boat. All of it. His concern for her safety.

"There's little point in staying here in New York," he stated. "Even though you and Korsak may have a workable scheme for cleaning up Rouard's mess, the administration is ignoring it. There are even rumors that the President is trying to persuade Congress to stop funding UNACC entirely. Bad publicity. Guilt by association, thanks to Rouard. And look how the public is reacting to the rest of the news about the dust cloud. I certainly misjudged the whole situation."

Indeed, news of the dust cloud in space had produced far more discord and panic in the United States than anyone could have imagined possible. Everyone was calling for Arab blood. The bastards had even duped the President and the Congress of the United States, however that was possible. How could such a thing be allowed to happen to the world. Someone should have been aware of what was going on, someone should have prevented it from happening. How dare they let the Arabs put all that dust into the upper atmosphere? Hadn't the first round of Kuwaiti oil field fires forty years ago been bad enough? And who had precipitated that mess? Old, then President, George, whatever his name was, that's who. And why hadn't he finished dealing with those assholes way back then? Why hadn't he gone in and stomped the hell out of them and wiped them off the face of the earth while he had a chance and been over and done with it? Then this wouldn't have happened, goddammit. It didn't matter that up until now no one seemed to care. Why should they? What could they have done about it? Finicky old mother earth anyway, falling apart like that, unable to compensate for man's desire to live a little too luxuriously. Shame, shame.

It wasn't the people's fault, that's for sure. Nature was just so damned quirky. But this, this dust cloud, now that was real. Those fucking Arabs had done it, and that son-of-a-bitchin

Frenchman who used to work for UNACC, funded in most part by the government of the United States. What a betrayal. That was real bullshit, taking advantage of the situation like that. Someone should have been aware of what was going on there, all right. Someone should have prevented it from happening. Where the hell was the Central Intelligence Agency, the National Security Council, the Army, the Navy, the Air Force and the Marines

All the anger and frustration of the foregoing years was pouring out. And now it had a focus. God bless America. It was time to destroy the middle east once and for all.

Meanwhile, Sam was doing his best to convince Jill it was time to get away from the east coast. There was little or nothing they could do there that would in any way have an impact, now that Rouard had done what he had done. And as twisted as some people's thinking was, Jill might even end up being blamed for part of it because of her previous association with the man and with UNACC.

"If things settle down a bit, we can always come back," he told her. "And just in case things really get bad, I'd feel more comfortable if the boat were ready and we had an able group of companions."

"I see your point," Jill said. "But who would you want to include and what do you think I should bring with me?"

They discussed it. "I'd like to have Korsak and Schalla come too," Sam said. "If you have no objections."

"To the contrary. I was hoping you would include them."

"Korsak is a very capable person."

"So is Schalla, or didn't you know?"

"Know what?"

"She was a real rebel when she was young. She wandered around your western states for a couple of years with an activist group of environmentalists living in the woods, knocking down power lines, using her daddy's allowance to buy supplies and equipment for raiding parties. I think she'd do very well in a survival situation."

"Schalla?"

"Schalla."

"For christsake. How did you find that out?"

"When women get together, they talk."

"We used to talk. She never told me."

"I can imagine what you two used to talk about."

"No we didn't. Why, are you jealous?"

"Not in the least."

"Why not?"

"Because I trust you. And because I know our relationship is different."

"It is. I love you."

"And I love you. So let me help? Do you want me to ask them if they'll come or are you going to tell them your plan first?"

"I wasn't going to. I wanted my friend Sheckman to meet them first, since we're partners in this thing."

"What about me?"

"There he doesn't have any choice."

As for agreeing to come west, Korsak had been the most eager but Schalla had required considerable coaxing. She felt the same as Jill had originally felt. Los Angeles was Los Angeles. Why would any sensible person want to go there, let alone a New Yorker? Once they arrived on the west coast however, she became quite comfortable with it. Sam had immediately contacted Sheckman to arrange a gathering so everyone could meet.

It was an old house, hidden far back from the road behind sycamore and cypress and oleander and bougainvillea. A single story ranch dwelling with a sprawling living room towards the rear that opened outward onto a large covered patio. The rest of the attendees were quite prompt as was to be expected from the carefully selected, but otherwise un-informed, group. The party began in a very unstructured way with cocktails and hors d'oeuvres, letting things take their course as Sam, Nate and Nate's wife paid particular attention as to how well everyone mingled with each other.

Jill had been talking to the Jackson's but was watching Sam as he spoke with Zhang, the young Chinese from Hong Kong. Suddenly, she had the urge to be at his side. She excused herself and went to him. Sam smiled and put his arm around her. She whispered in his ear. "I'm horny again."

"Me too," he said and kissed her on the nose.

"Isn't she lovely?" he said to Zhang.

"Yes, she is much so. Like my Chen who is from Shanghai."

"Chen is very beautiful," Jill said. "How did you meet?"

"I was in China helping to set up an electronics laboratory. She was in charge of the engineers there."

"Such an interesting group of people," Jill said.

"Yes," said Zhang, a very observant person. "Already I have met the doctor, a builder, a mechanical engineer, a horticulturist and two atmospheric scientists."

"Quite a variety all right. There is also an expert in agriculture, one in animal husbandry, a marine biologist, you and Chen who are specialists in electronics and that lady over there in the blue dress is a singer, songwriter and musician. Who did we leave out?"

"The Doctor's wife," Zhang said. "She is the psychologist who administered some rather unusual tests to us. I wonder why that was? Were there special qualifications necessary to be invited to this party?"

Sam laughed heartily as Bud and Jean came up to them. Everyone said hello again. "I heard about your difficult cross country trip," Jill said to them.

"It had it's moments," Bud agreed as Jean went on to entertain them with some of the highlights.

Deanna came by with drink in hand and said quietly to Sam. "What do you think?"

"You did a damned fine job Deanna. I like them all."

"Thought you might," she said. "Think we could all live together?"

"Sadly to say, it's beginning to look like we might get a chance to find out."

The guests were allowed to circulate freely for over two hours, something not nearly long enough for most of them. Then they sat down to dinner at an improvised, exceedingly long table heaped with a variety of dishes and spent another two hours lingering over food and conversation. It was here that Jean had asked Sam about the Arab involvement in the dust cloud episode

"It wasn't totally clear why they were being blamed," Jean said. "Is there more to it that you weren't allowed to print."

All eyes were on Sam. "It's not totally clear that they were directly involved at all," he said. "Off the record, however, I'd say someone there probably was. That's not provable, however, but, bottom line, I think the story was used as a cover up to protect other people, most of them in our own administration."

"Like who? The President?"

"Among others, yes."

"My god. Really?"

"Unfortunately, yes."

"Oh dear," Jean said. But I thought you had written the article."

"I wrote the original. What appeared in the paper was a highly distorted version with lots of implications that I would never have made. Then, to make it worse, they changed the headline and put my name to it."

"That's terrible. Isn't there anything you can do?"

"Not at this point," Sam said. "I thought I was onto something helpful just before I went to the South Pacific but my source seems to have vanished. For the second time."

Someone asked what he meant. He told them about Jed's disappearance and the unknown informant who never recontacted him.

"Do things like that really happen?" the same person asked.

"More than I'd like to think."

"Do you know who else was involved?" was the question that came from the far end of the table.

"I'm quite sure," he said. "But it would be risky to go into it at this time. It's also a very long story. I know that sounds like a put off, but it's not meant to be."

The subject was dropped and the conversation quickly changed to other topics. Then, after dessert and the third round of coffee, Sheckman rose and addressed the group.

"An official welcome to our home," he said and raised his wine glass in salute. Everyone returned the toast. "Now, as your doctor and the one partially responsible for bringing you all together," he continued, "and at the request of my good friend and collaborator, Sam Gorhman, I am going to prescribe what I think will be some very good medicine for us all." He paused.

"You are all invited to go on a shakedown cruise off the coast this weekend on our recently refurbished sail boat so that we might still get some sun while there's still some around. Can you all stand that?" He stopped and let the invitation hang in the air. Everyone seemed excited with the prospect. "Is there anyone who can't make it?"

"Darn, we were going up to Fresno to see the Barnards," Delores said.

"We'll call them and cancel," her husband, Bob, the architect, builder, jack of all trades stated.

Instructions were then given as to the time and how to find where the boat was moored. The party broke up shortly thereafter. The last to leave were Schalla, Korsak, Sam and Jill, all sharing Sam's house for the time being.

On the way home, Sam stopped at a bar and the four of them went for a drink. After they had ordered, Korsak said, "I didn't know you had a boat, Sam."

"It's mine and Sheckman's. We bought it nearly a year ago. It was an older model but with a sound hull and lots of optional gear aboard."

"It must be a decent size to be able to carry fourteen people for the weekend."

"Ninety five feet."

171

Korsak's eyebrows went up. "Ninety five feet?" he said in a dismayed tone. "You could live on that for months."

"That's exactly what I wanted to talk to you about," Sam said. "And we need to do it before the weekend."

"I see," Korsak said, quickly grasping what it was probably all about. "Did all that psychological testing I heard about tonight have something to do with it? It wasn't some little postgraduate research project of Deanna's at all, was it?"

"No, I'm afraid not."

"Why weren't Schalla and I asked to do this?"

"For the same reasons I wasn't," Jill said. "Sam had already pre qualified us."

"Pre qualified us for what?" Schalla asked. "What is going on?"

"I think you'd better tell them," Jill said.

Sam waited until their drinks were served, then began. It took him nearly half an hour to explain his thinking.

"But why a boat?" Korsak asked. "Why not a retreat in the mountains away from it all?"

"Two reasons. First, even as large as this country is, the wilderness areas that could support a group of people are much too small for the number of people who will have to try and live there. It would become much too dangerous, much too quickly. The oceans, on the other hand, are far more immense and there are thousands of remote islands we can put into. The number of sea worthy boats in the world compared to the population is limited and the ability of their owners to outfit and survive the seas for extended periods is even more limited. Sure, there will be pirates, but, barring just plain bad luck, we have every technological means necessary to avoid them. Should we have an encounter we may have to shoot first, which we will be prepared to do. Secondly, and possibly more important, the more the world situation deteriorates the higher the probability of nuclear war. Should that happen we stand a good chance of outrunning the radioactive fallout by being on the water."

"But how will you do that if you don't know where it's

likely to be at?"

"There are five global satellite networks still in existence. Hopefully at least one of them will remain in operation until such point as it doesn't matter anymore. Thanks to Zhang and Chen, we have the ability to monitor any of the five from almost anywhere on the globe. We will also have long and short wavelength radio, microwave and the deep water sonar communications channels. Somehow we should be able to gather the information we need. If we know where the activity is, I'm sure you and Jill will be able to predict any radioactive drift and recommend a safe path through it."

"Zhang and Chen are aware of your plans?"

"Yes. They only contracted to help with the electronics installations but they were are too damned smart not to know something was going on. And since there contribution was by far one of the most critical, I told them. And, if our weekend cruise works out, we'll ask the rest of the group if they want to participate."

"So the tests that Deanna had everyone take were compatibility tests?" Schalla said.

"That and a hell of a lot more. Compatibility, self esteem, verbal and nonverbal skills, initiative, problem solving abilities, flexibility, stress index, communication, determination, will power, philosophical outlook, and a few other things. All in all the tests were about two full days long. The very fact that these people were even willing and interested in taking them proved something. Deanna lost a lot of potential candidates right there."

"Whose idea was this?"

"What, the tests?"

"No, the boat, the survival scheme?"

"Originally? Mine, I guess."

"Sometimes you amaze the hell out of me Sam," Schalla said to him. "Does he you too?" she asked Jill.

"Him? No. Frankly I'm disappointed." Jill said as a tease.

"And what have I done to disappoint you, my luscious little creature?" Sam asked.

"I thought you probably had an interstellar spacecraft

hidden in the bushes behind your house. Something that could whisk us off to a peaceful little planet elsewhere in the galaxy."

"Of course. Super deluxe model fast enough to get us there in two days. Leave tomorrow, arrive Friday just in time for lunch. The test flight was scheduled for July but I ran out of funds. Sorry," he said and kissed her.

They sat looking at each other. "I love you," he said and hugged her. It was done openly and without embarrassment. There would be no secrets between the four of them, nor could there be from this moment on.

Sam continued. "I considered going up to Oregon and buying a forest so I could build an ark, too, but do realize how many animals there are in the world and how many trees I'd have to chop down to make a boat that big?"

"How did Noah do that anyway? His craft would have to have been bigger than Yankee Stadium?

"And how did he feed all those critters for forty days and forty nights and how did he keep the carnivores from eating the cows?"

"And who got stuck with clean up duty?" someone else asked after they ordered more drinks.

"Well," Sam said after they came. "We did the best we could. The only animals on board will be us."

"Luckily no one in the group has children to worry about."

"Not yet, anyway."

"And as for the rest of it, I'm glad you're here, Korsak, because I'd like to show you all the boat tomorrow and have you go over everything in detail in case we might have missed something. We can review the food supplies and perhaps do some thinking about social activities. And, damn. I forgot the most important thing."

"What is that?" Korsak asked.

"I didn't even ask you two if you wanted to come along. I just assumed you would. I had no right to do that."

Korsak looked at Schalla then back at Sam. "It wasn't necessary to ask. If it should come to that, we'll be there."

"Bravo," Schalla said. "Where this man goes, I go. To whatever end."

"Thank you," Sam said. "If it happens, we should have an excellent chance. We have an exceptional range of skills, talents and personality types."

"Did you plan the racial mix?"

"No. It just worked out that way. Two blacks, two Mexicans, a Native American, two Chinese, a Russian, an Australian and an odd assortment of gringo's."

"What is a gringo?" Korsak wanted to know.

Sam explained, then raised his glass. "To good friends and good company," he said. "Let's hope things improve. Then we can use the boat for some jaunts down the Mexican coast, instead, and maybe a trip to Hawaii."

"Why not Australia," Jill wanted to know.

"To Australia," everyone toasted.

They spent the next two days aboard the boat reviewing equipment, supplies and stores, plans, contingency plans, procedures, precautions, backup measures, filing in the gaps and generating a lengthy shopping list in the process, working late into the night, catching a few hours sleep on deck under the stars. What few that were still visible through the troubled atmosphere of Los Angeles.

Zhang and Chen came around the second day and went through a complete checkout of all the electronic gear aboard. The satellite monitors, the radar, sonar, ship to shore radio, microwave receivers, direction finders, backup and redundancy items, everything. And then they went through the store of spare parts and added to it. The twin diesel engines were started and the sails run up and down. Lines and blocks and cleats were inspected. The women cooked in the galley and examined the staterooms and heads for linens, towels and dispensables until foot by foot the entire vessel had been gone over. On the third day they fanned out across town to find all the items on the shopping list.

THIRTY

The second middle eastern coalition meeting had just gotten under way. It was seven days after the first one and took place in the same Tehran location. Unknown to the group at that moment in time, however, a multi stage missile had been launched but seconds before from an underground silo twenty five miles due east of Pretoria in South Africa. The liquid fueled projectile rose majestically from the earth in a northbound arc, dropped its first stage somewhere in the jungles of Zambia and the second stage in the hot sands of Sudan. The final stage, sedately identified with the South African flag on the exterior, began its reentry into the atmosphere.

If there had been passengers aboard, they would have had a brief but magnificent view of the entire middle east spread out below, before the nose cone opened like the petals of a large flower greeting the morning sun and discharged its five separate, fifty megaton warheads out in five different directions. It was a MIRV, a multiple insertion reentry vehicle, carrying five little presents that began to make their way downward, precisely and swiftly, one for each major nation of the coalition.

The coalition leader meanwhile had just risen to his feet and walked to the window, where he stretched himself, trying to make a point when there was a blinding flash directly overhead, followed immediately by a concussion wave that literally pounded the entire center of the city into the ground before the heat turned it into molten jelly that extended several feet down.

By the time the shock wave had expanded outward, leveling concrete structures more than twenty miles away from ground zero, most of the once living were already dead. Gamma rays, X-rays, neutrons, protons, electrons and an ensemble of other atomic particles had already violated the tissues of their bodies. And if that wasn't adequate enough, the thermal wave that followed shortly behind would finish the job.

Further out, a few would survive. For a while. Before

176

long, however, they would have a great envy for the quick fate of their brethren as unbelievable agony overcame their own bodies. Radiation poisoning, the ultimate by product of scientific brain cells gone awry. Glory be to the cleverness of man.

The Pentagon situation room was a flurry of activity. Reports had already begun to come in by the time General Simms burst into the room still dressed in civilian suit and tie from the party he had been attending. Colonel Stevens immediately came up to him and greeted him gravely.

"What's our status?" Simms asked.

"Full alert as ordered, sir."

"Has the President been informed?"

"He's standing by at the White House."

"Give me an update."

"Satellite imagery confirms a single launch point so it must have been a MIRV. Five separate warheads about fifty megatons each. Damascus, Tehran, Bagdad and Constantinople are totaled. Amman reports a few survivors but nothing appears to be left standing.

"Has the launch point been confirmed?"

"South Africa."

"Good god. Those bastards. Have they been warned?"

"Yes. But no acknowledgment."

"What do the byproducts look like? Do we know yet?"

"Old style warheads. Very dirty stuff with long half lives."

"Son-of-a-bitch. Can we re-target one of our own and reach them if we have to?"

"The NATO site in Spain is doing that now. They are standing by."

"But nothing from South Africa?"

"Negative, but the Israelis are demanding to know who the aggressor is."

"They don't know yet?"

"No sir. Their early warning system was off line, undergoing updates."

"Poor bastards. They're located dead center. Not too likely to survive all the fallout, I wouldn't think."

"What message should we relay?"

"Stall. We need to hear from the Africans."

THIRTY ONE

"Sam, Sam," Jill almost shouted.

"What's wrong?" Sam asked as he came into the study where Jill was watching the news, something one or both of them did almost round the clock anymore.

"Someone just blew up the middle east with nuclear weapons."

Too shocked to reply, Sam sat down beside her and listened as the report continued. Obviously, none of the specific details were all that clear as yet and much of it seemed speculative but none of it detracted from the awesome truth of what had happened and how suddenly and dramatically the entire world had been placed in severe danger. A danger where, if things should escalate, not only humans but all life forms would be in serious jeopardy.

The "live" report continued, sifting and re sifting the few facts which had actually been confirmed. That and telephone interviews with scientific and political experts, along with newscaster's speculations took more than an hour before the announcement was made that the President was now coming on the air to speak to the "American People."

"Well, at least he doesn't look as disgusting on the screen as he does in person," Jill commented as the man began to speak, obviously reading from a prepared speech on the teleprompter. A speech full of false humility, faked concern for the victims and a declaration of war against the aggressor. And finally, after his blathering was over, he added that in the best interest of the country and for the safety of all its citizens, he was declaring a national emergency. The entire National Guard had been called into active duty and Martial Law was now in effect.

"Exactly the excuse he was looking for," was all Sam could say at the moment, one of his worst fears now coming true. Then, almost as if right on cue, the leaders of seven different large, home grown militia groups, all from different parts of the country, called the station and made it clear that National Guard troops had damn well better stay the hell away from their territories or they would have a real war on their hands. The network station in turn then made a "live" call to the White House to see what the response would be but was told that the president was in a staff meeting and unavailable.

"What happens now?" Jill asked with concern. What did martial law really mean and why was it necessary, she wanted to know after giving Sam a chance to cool down a bit.

He explained it as best he could, saying he was not that surprised. It was a power grab by the president. Being commander in chief he had literally just given himself almost all the powers of a dictator. Except.......

"Except what?"

"Except I think he has badly misjudged the situation."

"How so?"

"For one thing, the militia. Estimates have it that their membership has increased at least ten times in the last five years alone. And while they are not all united as yet, they are all extremely well armed, probably fairly well trained and could easily come together as a whole. Not only that but Americans in general, personally own a lot of guns. Assault rifles, automatic weapons, you name it, they have it. That ego maniac is not going to keep the peace, he is going to destroy the country instead."

"Meantime, what?"

"Retaliation against South Africa by some middle eastern country. Also nuclear. Plus growing anarchy here at home."

"God, Sam. It seems so unreal. All our concerns about global warming and the ozone layer seem so minor in comparison. What do we do now?"

"It was a mistake not to have told the rest of our group the whole story at the party but I thought we would have had more time to check them out a little further first. Now it seems critical that we move ahead."

"What do you want me to do?"

"Take the other phone," he said as he dug a list of numbers out of his desk drawer, checked three of them and handed it to her. "Tell them we want them all to come to the boat this evening and that it's urgent. We'll explain when they get here."

THIRTY TWO

Unfortunately the South Africans were not about to openly acknowledge their hand in the deadly deed nor were the Israelis about to be stalled. They were in extreme jeopardy as evidenced and typified by a survival shelter in Tel Aviv. The dimly lit, concrete lined hole in the earth was grossly overcrowded. Some of the inhabitants could only sit in shock and stare. The calmer ones wept while others chanted and prayed in despair. Many were sick and the place was already beginning to reek, both from vomit and the foul perspiration of fear.

Outside a horde of people were beating on the closed, locked and sealed door that led into the shelter, wailing, "Let us in, let us in."

At the edge of the crowd a bent old man watched and listened in silence. Finally he turned and shuffled away, out into the empty street, head bowed in resignation, defeated and without hope. Tragic as the scene was, there was an even more sinister and threatening event in the making in the underground Israeli command center thirty kilometers east of Tel Aviv. A situation brought about by what was occurring above ground in almost every part of the country.

Seated in the conference room were Generals Ben Amin and Kadir and Captain Assir from the military sector, Mr. Gold, Vice Premier to the President and a Dr. Kublitz, chief scientific staff advisor. The President had been the unfortunate victim of a recent coronary and was unable to attend. He was still under treatment in a shelter near Jerusalem.

180

Large windows separated the conference room from the launch control center and the meeting attendees could see a flurry of activity in progress in the adjoining area. Readiness activity that would be normal under the present circumstances.

Dr. Kublitz was giving an update. "Radiation levels in Tel Aviv are fifty times normal and climbing. In the north it is even worse and the cloud from the Libyan bomb has yet to reach us."

"A serious situation," Mr. Gold said as General Kadir laughed sarcastically at the gross understatement.

"Dire," said Dr. Kublitz, being more respectful. "Radioactivity is in the air, in the dust and in the water supply. It is no longer safe to eat, drink or to breath."

"What about the shelters?" Gold asked.

"Capacity for two hundred thousand total, nationwide. Most with less than two weeks of supplies."

"Can we evacuate?"

"In contaminated planes and boats? Even if some survived the trip, who in their right mind would let us in?"

"Have the Americans informed us of the aggressor as yet?"

"Damn the Americans. They think they are safe. What do they care?"

"Not so safe with the clouds moving. Sooner or later they will share the radioactivity with the rest of the world."

"Good, but not good enough. Fortunately we do not need them any longer."

"You know the strike origin?" Gold asked.

"The Bloemfontein complex in South Africa," Captain Assir said.

Totally taken aback, Gold could only sit and stare at him.

"Obviously they thought we were expendable in the process," General Kadir said.

"And before we are all dead, I suggest we launch and return the good deed, both to them and the Americans," replied General Ben Amin.

"What are you talking about?" Gold said in a shocked voice. "The Americans? How could you even consider such a

181

thing?"

"Very easily," said Ben Amin coldly. "Pretoria, Johannesburg and Cape Town are already targeted and locked in. So is Washington DC.. We will not go over the North Pole with the first one, but straight west. And, since it is highly unlikely the Americans will be expecting something from that direction, we stand a good chance of getting through their early warning system. Just in case however, there will be another one close behind from farther north. Let them wonder if it came from Moscow."

"Are you insane? What have the Americans to do with it?"

"Everything, as it turns out. If Israel has nothing else it has the best intelligence network in the world. We have been informed by our operatives in Washington of a project called Gray Sky. The Americans were the ones who initiated and funded the dust cloud mission of Dr. Rouard's."

"I don't believe it. And besides, you cannot retaliate in such a way. It's inhuman. I will not allow it."

"You are the final authority?" Ben Amin scoffed.

"That responsibility has been delegated to me, yes."

"Then we will proceed without you."

"I will not give you the clearance code.

Ben Amin nodded at the Captain. "Captain Assir is from cryptography. He already has it."

Mr. Gold came to his feet in anger. "I will not let you do this. You are in direct violation of the President's orders."

General Kadir also rose and sided with Mr. Gold. "He is right. You cannot do this," he said but as he spoke Ben Amin again nodded at Captain Assir. Assir got to his feet and took a step towards the control room but was immediately blocked by Gold and the General. Not only was it the same moment that Sam had first welcomed his last two guests aboard the boat, it was the same moment when Ben Amin withdrew his pistol and pointed it at General Kadir and Mr. Gold back in Israel. "Would you like to die now or cling to a few more days with the rest of us?" he asked them.

"You're insane," Gold shouted at him.

"How unique," Ben Amin smiled. "The only one of my kind in the whole world. Now get out of the way."

Gold and Kadir stared at him through the silence in the room. After a calculated wait Ben Amin said, "You may proceed Captain."

Captain Assir stepped around the two men who blocked his path, went into the control room and spoke to one of the personnel at the master control station. The man moved aside and Assir entered something into the keyboard. Five green lights came on in the display panel. He made a second entry. The five green lights were replaced by five blinking red lights. At this point Mr. Gold turned and began running towards the control room door. Ben Amin dropped him in his tracks with a silenced but well placed round directly between the shoulder blades just as Captain Assir began pushing the fire control buttons in sequence. Washington DC first, the backup second and South Africa one, two and three immediately thereafter. It was now very nearly exactly forty eight hours after the lights had gone out in Tehran, Amman, Tehran, Tripoli and Constantinopal.

THIRTY THREE

At the same time that Captain Assir got to his feet to obey Ben Amin's order, the last pair of Sam's guests arrived at the boat and were welcomed aboard, everyone still very shocked at what had happened to the five Arab countries in the middle east two days before. They were also growing somewhat more concerned with what was going on in their own country. But what, if anything, did Sam have to do with any of it, those who hadn't as yet been given the entire scenario? He was just an investigative reporter. Or had been, anyway. Maybe he was canceling their weekend getaway boat ride and taking them out for a cruise in the moonlight. Now that would be nice. Set worry and concern aside for a few hours. But if it was just that, why all the urgency?

Having been welcomed at the dock, they were all brought into the large stateroom below deck. All except for Dr. Sheckman. He had left earlier to drive up to Santa Barbara to pick up one last load of medical supplies he felt necessary for the boat and wouldn't return for three or four hours. The rest were all offered a drink and asked to sit so Sam could tell those that didn't already know, what the real purpose was for bringing them together.

Beginning, he explained his and Sheckman's concept of the mission in detail and what might be necessary to survive if the international situation got any worse. Then he stopped and answered questions. Lots of questions. One of them was where would they sail to.

"Mainly the mid Pacific. There, we have thousands and thousands of square miles of ocean containing thousands of small to medium sized islands we can check out. If need be, we can go even farther. Above all, the primary purpose is to avoid the radioactive fallout. But we will also still stay away from places where there is any population density. Coastal cities, resort areas, anywhere there is pending danger from the dust clouds or nuclear fallout. Since people there will feel trapped, someone may well choose to take our boat by force and that we cannot allow. I know it might be hard not being able to mingle with other human beings for long periods of time, but better to be on a ghost ship than to lose our one hope of survival, especially if the war escalates. Ultimately, of course, our biggest and most difficult challenge may well be with ourselves. Keeping our own sanity here aboard the boat if it comes to that, and, getting along with each other long term in this limited and difficult situation."

More questions were asked and to answer some of the more important, they went on a tour of the boat and ended in the control room. Here Sam explained key features of their electronics capability. Primarily the ability to listen.

"Listen to what?" someone asked.

"To ground based and satellite relayed information. Television and full spectrum radio. We are also able to listen in on the U.S. Navy's extremely low frequency sonar communications which might prove valuable at some point. All of this will help us decide where, and where not, to go."

An hour went by. One hour became two and two became three. Then the biggest question of all. A year ago, maybe even just a few months ago, the entire thing would have been dismissed by several members of the group as nothing more than some idle, crazy scheme put together by a pair of paranoid fools. But now, with five nuclear bombs having already been dropped on the middle east, my god...

"At what point would you consider it serious enough to leave?"

"It depends on what happens next. If there is retaliation and, who it is that retaliates. And most definitely if there is an attack on the U.S. mainland. Or, barring that, as soon as the internal structure of this country begins to collapse."

"Is that really a danger?" Schalla asked.

"Yes," said Sam. "I seriously believe it is."

"But how can you be so sure that any of that will happen," Bill the architect asked. "Is there something the public doesn't know?"

"There are lots of things none of us know about. Maybe I'll never get a chance to prove it but one thing I do know is that the President, and others from this country, were somehow involved in the dust cloud scheme."

"What? What is there to be gained from doing that?"

"A lot, if you are as crazy as he seems to be. As you know, not only is the President extremely nationalistic and imperialistic both, I think he is also delusional."

"Delusional? About what?"

"His own importance for one thing."

"We know that. He's the world's biggest bully. An extreme sociopath. How he got elected is beyond me."

"Yes, but it goes even further. Remember how he proposed invading Mexico when he first took office. And all his war mongering statements to China and Russia? And several countries in Africa."

"Sure, but why Africa?"

"Resources. Rare metals needed in the electronics and automotive industries. Plus, some of the statements he denies having made. The ones about the poorer nations."

"I don't remember. Like what?"

"About people starving to death. He said, 'If we have to feed them, we don't need them.'"

"Are you sure? I thought it was .... My god. So..."

"So, in his eyes there is a lot to gain by speeding up the process."

"The southern hemisphere dust clouds. But what about Australia and all those other countries?"

"Some are just peripheral damage. Others, like Brazil and Argentina are also sitting on some of the world's largest deposits of precious metals and other resources. Undoubtedly, he was also behind the guerrilla warfare there. Partly for real and partly to implicate the Arabs later on. As for Russia, he seriously wanted that to succeed, which it was because the central government is still so weak after their revolution tore it all apart."

"And it's too far north to risk putting a dust cloud over it because it might drift over North America."

"Yes. But what the president and his little group of conspirators didn't seem to realize is that it's too risky to put up such huge dust clouds anywhere. Even if they don't drift, blocking sunlight in the southern hemisphere alone is going to put us on the verge of an ice age if the dust cloud particles don't start bunching up and precipitating out rather quickly. The effects of that alone will end the lives of many more millions of people."

"The poor bastards."

"Exactly. And now the bombs in the middle east. No wonder everyone is crazy with fear. But what's going to happen when the real truth comes out? When it becomes clear that our own president has to have been involved?" Sam asked and stopped, letting the full impact of his words sink in, not as yet knowing what hidden cameras in other parts of the country would already be showing.

In Cleveland the local police were exchanging gunfire with a band of looters that had holed up in a downtown department store. In Madison, Wisconsin a group of dissident university students were inside the state capitol carefully placing dozens of sticks of dynamite in strategic structural locations of the building. In Brooklyn there were still over five thousand demonstrators in the streets at three o'clock in the morning setting cars and buildings on fire. The National Guard had formed a line and had been ordered to open fire if the crowd refused to end its march of destruction.

On a shabby street corner in Hollywood a destitute couple shuffled along. The woman stopped at the news rack, read the headlines which asked, *Is The End In Sight*, and began to cry loudly.

"Stop your goddamned crying for chrissake," the man shouted at her. "All you do anymore is cry, cry, cry. You're driving me goddamned crazy, goddammit."

A little further down the street a young man with greasy long hair and filthy clothes was preaching on the sidewalk.

"Repent," he shouted. "Give up your sins, come to the lord now. Come into the fold before we are all doomed..."

Two young toughs in leather and chains laughed derisively as they passed him on their way to the bar on the opposite side of the street. They gave him a poke and tried to snatch his bible away. The preaching one pulled back, saving his good book but slipped and fell off the curb. He got up and shouted after them. "The lord will punish you for your sinful ways."

The tormentors stepped out into the street in front of the traffic and made their way across and into the barroom. The barroom was large, dingy and full of smoke. It also smelled of vomit and stale beer. Nearly everyone inside was drunk. The bar itself ran along the full length of the greater wall with people two and three deep against it. Off in an L-shaped room to the side, a large ring of men sat in a circle watching a couple on a chair in the center of the group. The man was seated with his pants down around his ankles. The girl had her dress pulled up and was astride, riding him. The man gasped and let out a big moan. The crowd cheered. Someone said loudly, "fourteen down and twenty left to go."

Two girls from the bar wandered over as the girl got off, still holding up her dress. The man pulled up his pants and another sat down and took his place. The first girl observer said, "she's nuts, screwing all those assholes. Nobody likes sex that much."

"Oh, I don't know," said her friend. "Maybe she's got the right idea."

"Yeah, what?"

"She said she'd rather fuck herself to death than die of radiation poison."

They were both interrupted by a scream from near the front door as the young man who had been preaching across the street came in shouting and waving a pistol.

"Damn you sinners all to hell. How dare you blasphemize the name of the Lord, thy God," he shouted and fired a round into the ceiling.

Drunk as they were, most of the crowd dropped instinctively to the floor. The circle off to the side parted quickly as most of the spectators broke and ran, exposing the couple in the middle, still engaged but too surprised and shocked to react. The young man spotted them and approached, shouting all the more. "Fornication is the greatest of all sins," he yelled. "As God's messenger I tell you there is no redemption for such mockery," and with that he emptied the pistol into their bodies, killing them both.

There was more scenarios similar to this one, also. A lot more, all across the country as law and order began to unravel out of panic and fear, slowly at first, but growing. Something which most of Sam's guests were relatively unconcerned with as yet, just as they were still totally unaware of what else had already happened almost three hours earlier on the other side of the country, isolated as they had been below deck on the boat. It was only when some of them were getting ready to go home that Sam realized he hadn't heard from Sheckman since he had left earlier. But, where was his cell phone? Damn, he had left it in his and Jill's cabin.

Sam cursed again when he had the phone in his hand and realized that Sheckman had already tried to call several times.

"Is everything okay," he asked Sheckman, once Sheckman answered.

"So far," was the answer. "What have you been doing? Are you okay. I tried to call several times."

"I know. I'm sorry. I was with the group and forgot my phone. Where are you at now.?"

"On the way back. Just coming into Malibu. I think I'll be okay but jesus.."

"What's wrong?"

"Panic. For god's sake, Sam. Turn the TV on. Then call me back."

It was the same disorganized chaos on every channel. Panels of newscasters, some looking stunned and almost unable to speak, others weeping openly, unable to stop. Then, what had to be an ongoing repeat of a series of pictures of the destruction. It had been early evening when the bombs hit, both within the Highway 495 beltway in Washington, DC.. First, snapshots taken of the mushroom clouds from a distance separated in time by about two minutes, the picture taker probably near death by now, having had to have been exposed to the first streams of deadly radiation given off by the blasts to get the shots. Then, more pictures of the aftermath. Clearly, there was no White House, no Capital Building, no Washington Monument, no Supreme Court, no Smithsonian, no Pentagon, nothing at all. Nothing but flattened landscape and rubble for miles and miles and miles, much of it still smoldering and on fire. And to the east, farther out, there was no Andrews Air Force Base either. Or a Fort Belvoir to the south, or Fairfax to the west. And to the north most of the city of Rockville was in ruins.

No wonder people were crying, the ones who had been spared. As for the near dead, the victims of the radiation, the blast and the heat, they were probably in far too much agony to even do that. And then, finally some pictures taken after the sun went down, which, except for the light from a few fires still dotting the landscape in the distance, there was nothing, nothing but darkness. And then, the final irony. An announcement just as Sam was about to go back up on deck and call Sheckman again.

"We have just learned from officials at Camp David, Maryland that the president and key members of his staff were on their way to the retreat at the time of the first explosion. Unfortunately, the presidential helicopter and two others were airborne and at an altitude and heading that would have placed them all, almost at the dead center of the first blast when it went off. Additionally, the only other officials of government that have been heard from far are Secretary of State Robert Mulldowny who was in Japan at the time and the junior congressman from Iowa, Willburt Ames, who is in a Des Moines hospital recovering from a hernia operation. We will....."

THIRTY FIVE

"Holy Christ," was all Sam could say when Sheckman answered.

"For sure."

"Where are you at?"

"Lower Malibu now. Maybe ten minutes if I can get through."

"Why, what's wrong?"

"Panic. There are a million cars on the road. Looks like people are afraid L.A. might be the next target. Fortunately most of them are on the other side of the highway going north but some of them have started spilling over into the southbound lanes."

"Will you be all right?"

"I hope so. And, I do you have the supplies."

"Good, but leave them behind if you have to."

"Of course. When do you want to leave?"

"As soon as you can get here. Stay on the line and keep me posted."

Enough bad news, everyone was up on deck by then, men in shock, women crying, several on the verge of panic. Then, in the distance, sounds of gunfire.

"It's started," Sam said.

"What?" asked Jill.

"The doomsday hysteria. Mass craziness, shooting in the streets."

"Are we safe until Nate gets here?"

"Probably wouldn't hurt to get some guns up here."

"I'll go," Bud said.

"Me too," said Korsak. "I know where they're at."

"Bring rifles and handguns both."

Damn, Sam said to himself, as Sheckman kept up a running commentary on his progress. He was now coming down Pacific Avenue towards the marina area.

"Okay, now I'm on West Washington almost to Bora Bora Avenue. Oh, hell. What's this? Looks like a blockade."

"A blockade? Where?"

"On Bora Bora. L.A. County Sheriffs. They're not letting anyone into the harbor."

Two minutes later Sheckman was back. "Tahiti and Marquesas are also blocked so Via Marina probably is too. Yeah, it sure is. What's this all about?"

"The marina is where the mayor and half the power brokers in the city have their yachts berthed. Problem is they're probably too late. There's already some gunfire not too far from here so if you get through, be ready."

"And if I can't, then what?"

"How many deputies at the blockade?"

"As near as I can tell, three."

"Okay. Stay put. Korsak and I will drive over and wait on this side. And we'll be armed, too. Somehow we'll get you through."

"Right. But let me try it my way first. I'm a doctor,

191

remember? I'm sure I can think of something."

Sam pulled his car over and parked a hundred yards down from the barrier and waited with the lights out.

The sheriff's vehicle, lights on, had been backed up onto the curb and blocked a portion of the pavement. The rest was barricaded with yellow and black saw horses. Two uniformed deputies stood with their backs to Sam and Korsak on the far side of the barricade facing the direction of Sheckman's car which, by now, had made it up to the site where the third deputy was talking to Sheckman through his rolled down window. Sheckman's phone was still on and they could hear parts of the conversation as the deputy interrogated him. It took a while. Then the deputy handed back Sheckman's license, shined his light in the rear seat and motioned to the other two.

"Dammed if it didn't work," Nate said into his phone after he was through. "I'm on my way."

"We know," Sam said as he turned his car lights back on and blinked them a few times. "Go on past us. We'll turn around and follow you in."

A block away from the boat Sheckman screeched to a halt again, a matter of several yards away from a line of hard looking men on motorcycles strung across the road under the streetlight as Sam pulled up alongside where they rolled down their windows so they could talk.

"What do you think they want?" Sheckman asked.

"A boat. It must be obvious to them that we have one or we wouldn't be here."

"You're probably right. Looks like they're armed, too,"

"I noticed," Sam said. "But just holstered handguns."

"What's good about that?" Sheckman wanted to know just as another line of men pulled up a ways behind them and also stopped.

"We'll see," Sam said and gave some instructions to Korsak. The he turned to talk to Sheckman again.

"Keep your head down," he yelled. "And be prepared to

go. We don't have time to waste messing with these scumbags," and with that Korsak and he both got out of their car at the same time, one facing the forward line of interlopers, one facing the rear. Their big rifles came up. They quickly aimed and fired. And then again as gas tanks exploded and the riders jumped off their machines and ran. It was enough. The rest of the mob burned rubber turning their bikes around and disappeared into the distance. All except one. He drew his weapon and aimed it at Sam. Too bad he was so slow. Korsak blew him clear off his machine long before he could pull the trigger and that was that.

THIRTY SIX

Sleek but silent as a shadow against the background noise of the city, the darkened craft slid through the channel under the well muffled power of one engine, leaving hardly a ripple behind in the calm surface. Once past the breakwater the sails began going up. Dark gray sails without numbers or emblems on them. Sails that soaked up the light and helped to camouflage the vessel. Sails that picked up the off shore breeze and took them out to sea.

Faster now, heading into the open water, they skirted Catalina Island, then turned southwest. If all went well they would be in the international zone by morning. And after that? What? Nothing but nameless, faceless uncertainty. Anxiety, fear, dread, worry, isolation, friends and family left behind. How would it all resolve itself and would they survive long enough to even find out? What had happened was as yet too vast and too overwhelming to completely embrace, leaving them with nothing left to do but sail off into the darkness and what lay beyond, hope sustaining them as best it could.